P9-AOF-132

SUMMER AT THE HAVEN

Also by Katharine Moore:

Victorian Wives
She for God: Aspects of Women and Christianity
The Little Stolen Sweep
Moog

SUMMER AT THE HAVEN

a novel by
KATHARINE MOORE

ALLISON & BUSBY
LONDON/NEW YORK

First published 1983
by Allison & Busby Limited,
6a Noel Street, London W1V 3RB, England,
and distributed in the USA by
Schocken Books Inc.,
200 Madison Avenue, New York, NY 10016

British Library Cataloguing in Publication Data:
Moore, Katharine
    Summer at the Haven.
    I. Title
    823′.94[F]   PR 6063.0

    ISBN 0-85031-511-5

Photoset in 12/14pt Times by
Derek Doyle & Associates, Mold, Clwyd
Printed in Great Britain by
Billings & Sons Ltd, Worcester

CONTENTS

To Josephine Fry

1

THE HAVEN

THE HAVEN, a private Home for elderly ladies, was by now not unlike its inmates, but it had originally been the proud achievement of a prosperous Victorian merchant who had pulled down the old Tudor farmhouse, once a Manor, and erected on its site a handsome structure in the fashionable pseudo-Gothic style with a side turret and stained-glass windows over the porch and on the stairs and even in the proud bathroom. His sons had been killed in the 1914 war, the family had faded out and the house, untenanted throughout the Second World War, had at length been sold off cheaply to be converted for its present purpose. It was thoroughly unsuitable for this, being just too far away from the large village of Darnley for convenience or company. Its rooms were big and had to be divided, which made them disproportionately lofty and a queer shape, and the menace of worn floors and windows and roof tiles was always present to the harassed house committee. It was also too secluded to attract domestic staff and there was not enough money available to tempt them by high wages.

The house made a brave effort, however, though this was never enough to achieve an all-over effect. Some sections peeled obviously away while others showed a distinct facelift and, where once there had been an elegant conservatory, a square annexe containing the offices, which looked rather as if it were constructed of cardboard, had been painted a bright pink.

The Victorian merchant had found nothing much in the way of a garden. There were a few old fruit trees growing out of a rough grass space ending in an ancient ditch, on the other side of which was a little copse of oak, ash and thorn. He had laid out a lawn and flowerbeds and, though he had left the old trees, he had planted near the house a monkey-puzzle and a deodar which had grown to fine proportions. As with the house, there was now a struggle to keep the most visible and utilitarian part of the garden trim and flourishing. The narrow beds each side of the gravel sweep were filled with neat bedding plants, begonias and geraniums in the summer, chrysanthemums and dahlias in the autumn. Spring bulbs were not encouraged because they were untidy. In fact, all the cultivated parts of the garden were rather like the shelves of a self-service store with rows of the same sort of goods kept orderly and separate. At the back of the house, a short strip of the old lawn was regularly mown and there were two beds of floribunda roses, one pink and one red. There was a small trimmed shrubbery of privet, laurel and lilac and, in a discreet corner, ranks of vegetables. Only under one window, was a plot where well tended but not very tidy flowers were happily mixed up together like the goods in an old-fashioned village shop.

The Haven, when full, could accommodate eight old ladies. Each had their own room containing their remnants of furniture, china and pictures. It also housed the warden and whatever resident staff that could be scraped together.

Mrs Thornton's room was the larger of the two attics. It had originally held three narrow iron bedsteads in which had slept a parlour maid, a housemaid and an underhousemaid. The smaller attic had been the cook's and was now used as a boxroom. Mrs Thornton had chosen her room because she did not like the sound of people tramping above her and because, as the other attic was empty, she felt an assurance of comparative privacy. The shape of the room, too, appealed to her – the interior of the absurd turret opened out of one corner – this had been where the parlour maid had slept, thus claiming her superiority over the other two maids, and Mrs Thornton in her turn had thought it very convenient for her own bed, which was the one on which her son had been born. From the little turret window she could see the railway line and the trains, now, alas, much depleted in number, that connected the branch station with the main line, seemed to her like a link with the outer world. The other window looked on to the front drive, used by whoever called in from this outer world. So, although the lift stopped short of the attic floor and it was cold there in winter and hot in summer and the sloping ceilings allowed little wallspace, she felt the advantages outweighed the disadvantages.

Besides her bed, she had brought with her her mother's rocking-chair and her husband's bureau, the gate-legged table they had bought together when furnishing their first home, and as many books as she could find room for. All these articles were thickly encrusted with memories. On the whole, if no longer happy, she was content. When tempted to indulge in melancholy she would take herself in hand and at such times she would hear the voice of her Scotch nanny quite clearly, as though she were in the room: "Count your blessings, Miss Milly." It was her favourite maxim and perhaps next came: "Eat up everything on your plate, now. I canna have a faddy bairn in my nursery. There's many a poor callant would be glad to have what you are wanting to leave each day." At the time, when suffering from some childish grief or lacking appetite – for she was a delicate little girl – Nanny seemed not only unsympathetic but stupid. Any other blessing but the one denied her then and there seemed quite unreal, and as for the unwanted dinner, how she wished the poor child would come and take it away from

11

her. But in old age and at The Haven, while more profound advice was forgotten, Nanny's precepts remained and stood her in good stead both at the rather unappetizing meal times and in moods of dejection.

One wet cold May morning, then, she began deliberately to count her blessings. She was not deaf like old Miss Brown, only a little hard of hearing; she was not going blind like old Miss Norton, only with gently failing sight; she was not crippled and wracked with arthritis like old Miss Dawson, only troubled at night by one hip and one knee; she was not bald like old Miss Ford underneath her wig, only going a little thin around the temples; she was not asthmatical and bronchial like old Mrs Perry; above all, unlike poor dear old Mrs Langley, she was still in her right mind; only proper names eluded her in a stupidly arbitrary manner. It was strange, she realized suddenly, that she was thinking of everybody as old when she herself was as old, or in some cases, even older than they. She must try to remember this. One other blessing occurred to her – her heart was not all that strong, unlikely, as in some cases she knew, to outlast the rest of her. She gave it all the work she could, walking up and down to her attic, for instance, disdaining the help of the lift for the first two floors.

She had got thus far in practising Nanny's maxim that morning when she was disturbed by a voice, not altogether unlike Nanny's own in tone, and when she was not at her best either. It was the voice of Miss Blackett, the warden, from the landing below.

"Mrs Langley, whatever are you doing?"

A foolish little laugh in reply floated up through Mrs Thornton's half-open door and then she heard another door firmly shut and Miss Blackett's steps ascending the stairs. The warden could only be called a mixed blessing and Mrs Thornton braced herself for the encounter. Hardly waiting to knock, Miss

12

Blackett marched into the room.

"Mrs Thornton, I wonder that with your door ajar you didn't hear Mrs Langley wandering about. I have just found her playing absolute havoc with the linen cupboard — sheets and towels all over the floor and herself actually standing on a pile of blankets trying to reach the upper shelves; and when I asked her what she was up to she said she was looking for her baby's clothes and that her husband was coming this afternoon to fetch them both. She thinks that this is a maternity home and that she's just had a child. She shouldn't really be here now and I don't think we can keep her any longer. She must go into the geriatric ward at the hospital."

"Oh, no!" exclaimed Mrs Thornton, "surely not, Miss Blackett. She is so happy and she never does any real harm, it is only that she doesn't live in the present any more. She believes her husband and the friends she has loved in the past come to see her every day — she never stops believing it and so of course they do."

Miss Blackett stared at her blankly and Mrs Thornton swore inwardly. Would she never learn not to make remarks like that to people like Miss Blackett? No, she supposed at her age she never would. It would almost certainly make it worse now if she went on, but go on of course she did.

"If she goes into a geriatric ward she will be treated like an invalid and she'll have to leave everything behind, all her things, I mean, and then she may wake up, you see."

"Well, wouldn't that be desirable," said Miss Blackett crossly, "though I fear it isn't at all likely, senility never regresses — and as to her things, she has far too many of them and she never dusts them."

Residents at The Haven, if able-bodied, were expected to do their own dusting. It gave them something to do and relieved the domestic situation just a little.

"She says that Susan, her housemaid, who has been with the family for years, sees to all that whenever I mention it," went on Miss Blackett, adding, with a rare touch of humour: "I only wish I could lay my hands on that Susan."

Immediately Mrs Thornton felt herself thaw and she noticed for the first time, too, how tired the warden looked and that she was leaning against the door as she talked.

"Isn't Brenda due back tomorrow?" she asked. Brenda was the latest living-in help and away for a week's holiday.

"She isn't coming back at all," said Miss Blackett. "She phoned last night that she's taken a job in a shop — too quiet here, she says. She didn't even have the decency to give in her notice."

Mrs Thornton looked distressed, she and the warden both belonged to the generation that expected a month's notice and could not easily accept modern casualness.

"Oh, dear, that leaves only Gisela and Mrs Mills," she said. Gisela was the au pair from Germany who was a recent arrival. Miss Blackett did most of the cooking herself. She was an adequate but not a good cook, not being interested in food. Mrs Mills, the gardener's wife, came in to do cleaning.

"Yes," sighed Miss Blackett, "I shall have to let the committee know and try advertising again, I suppose."

"I'll do Mrs Langley's dusting," said Mrs Thornton.

Miss Blackett merely sniffed in response, recalling Mrs Thornton's remarks about Mrs Langley with irritation. She had thought Mrs Thornton had more sense, but they were none of them to be relied on. She turned and went downstairs. Why ever Mrs Thornton chose to stay on in that attic when there was now a good room available on the second floor, she failed to understand. If she moved down the attic floor could be left to take care of itself, which would save a good deal more work than doing the dusting for Mrs Langley, who ought not to be here

14

any longer anyway. But none of them thought of anyone but themselves. The old were so self-centred.

After lunch and resting time were over, Mrs Thornton knocked on Mrs Langley's door. She had thought out her plan of action carefully and marched in flaunting her duster about and talking rather loudly and quickly.

"I know it is Susan's day out, Mrs Langley, and I wondered, as you are sure to be having visitors for tea, whether you would like me just to go over your lovely china so as to have everything looking just as it would if Susan were here."

Mrs Langley, who was in her nineties, was sitting by what should have been the fireplace but was now only a cold radiator, for the heating was turned off, it being May by the calendar though nearer November in temperature. She was a pretty old lady with large faded blue eyes and white curls done up with a narrow green velvet ribbon on the top of her head. Her face was singularly smooth and unlined. She was wrapped in a none too clean little grey shawl and Mrs Thornton's heart smote her as she saw it.

"Dear Jessie," said Mrs Langley, "how very kind."

She always called Mrs Thornton Jessie, but who Jessie really was she had never discovered. She preferred it, however, to her own name, for Milly, rhyming inexorably with silly, filly and frilly, had been unfortunate for her in her schooldays.

"I am expecting the vicar," went on Mrs Langley. "He said he'd come about the christening – not that he's likely to notice a little dust, gentleman don't, do they – but it's well, perhaps, to be on the safe side."

The lovely Chelsea shepherdess on the mantelpiece had the same slightly neglected, soiled look as her owner, but Mrs Thornton soon put her to rights and her attendant shepherd, too. Between them was a row of enchanting tiny china houses and a Dresden flower piece. But Miss Blackett was right, the room was

15

really too cluttered up with ornaments and furniture, and all the wallspace was completely covered with photographs in dark oak frames and pale watercolours in gilt ones. There were far too many chairs and small tables and they none of them seemed to know what they were doing or where they were meant to be. Yet Mrs Thornton was sure that everything in the room was significant and precious to Mrs Langley. She dusted them as carefully and quickly as she could and finished just as Gisela, the German girl, appeared with tea – a brown teapot, a plastic cup and a plate upon which were two slices of bread and butter and a dull little cake.

Mrs Langley clicked in disapproval. "Would you mind getting out the Worcester cups from my corner cupboard? My husband will be here directly, I always hear the carriage at about this time." She seemed to have forgotten the vicar by now. "My husband likes to drive himself, you know, though he brings James with him to hold Bessie and Brownie while he is here, such a dear fine pair they are."

Mrs Thornton found the cups and placed them on the tea tray where they looked sadly out of place. Such was the happy expectation in Mrs Langley's voice that she caught herself listening for horses and carriage wheels as she went upstairs to her own room. She did not hear them but she knew that Mrs Langley would.

Meanwhile Miss Blackett was having her own welcome cup in her office siting-room and making notes in preparation for the house committee meeting on the following day. These were held only quarterly unless a crisis arose needing immediate attention. On the whole, Miss Blackett enjoyed them. She was listened to with respectful attention when she gave her report, for the committee knew she would be difficult to replace.

"Granted that Miss Blackett is not the ideal warden," said the chairwoman, Lady Merivale, to her secretary, "but she is conscientious and hard-working and she is also cheap, which, I need hardly say, is a sad but inevitable necessity in these times." The secretary had been hinting that Miss Blackett seemed sometimes to lack sensitivity.

She had been a matron in a boys' preparatory school for some years but had then thought that old ladies might be easier to manage. She found she was mistaken. You generally knew where you were with small boys, but with "them", as she always thought of the old ladies, you never knew – they were so unreliable. "Unreliable" was her favourite term of disapproval. She bore "them" a grudge for the mistake she had made but she did not feel like another change.

Miss Blackett's room was the extreme opposite of Mrs Langley's. It was spotless and very neat, her papers stacked in tidy piles on her desk, on the top of which stood the one picture in the room, a small faded photograph of a kitten. Miss Blackett sat at her desk and wrote:

(1) Mrs Langley, to be removed to the geriatric unit of the hospital as soon as possible.
(2) The deodar tree to be cut down. It makes Miss Dawson's room very dark and also damp, as it is far too near the house and in wet weather its branches drip down the walls.
(3) Report on Brenda's leaving and discuss replacement.
(4) Report on repairs to gutters and bathroom pipe and request for repainting of front ground-floor window frames and needful repair of old stable door and lock.

As she finished the last note, a large ginger cat rattled imperiously at the door and was immediately let in. He sat down at once on the top of Miss Blackett's papers. She sighed resignedly and stroked him. This was Lord Jim, so christened by a Mrs Wilson, a late resident, the widow of a naval officer, who had read nothing but Conrad's novels and made his wife read them too. Miss Blackett knew nothing of Conrad and thought the name a compliment to her cat's proud manners. She was therefore pleased with the name. Everyone knew that Lord Jim could do no wrong in her eyes and everyone thought her one photograph was of him, but in this they were wrong. It was of her only childhood's pet, passionately loved but put to sleep when he reached maturity because the aunt who had brought her up said he ruined the furniture and harboured fleas. Miss Blackett could not believe that Lord Jim was not a privilege and pleasure for all the old ladies and good for them, too. This happened to be true as regards Mrs Thornton, Miss Norton and Miss Brown, but quite untrue of Miss Dawson and Mrs Perry. Mrs Perry's passion was flowers and she it was who lovingly tended that herbaceous border beneath her window. Unfortunately Lord Jim's favourite daybed was precisely on this plot. It was sunny and sheltered from cold winds and he enjoyed both sleeping there and trying to catch the butterflies that hovered over the lavender and pinks and buddleia.

"Lord Jim does love your little garden, Mrs Perry," said Miss Blackett approvingly. "He's made quite a nest for himself so cleverly there, do you see?"

Poor Mrs Perry did indeed see, but she said nothing for she knew the situation was hopeless both from Miss Blackett's point of view and Lord Jim's. As for Miss Dawson, her passion was for birds and ever since Lord Jim, with that inspired tactlessness not seldom to be observed in cats, had laid a dead thrush at the door of her room, there had been a bitter one-sided feud between her and the warden – one-sided because Miss Blackett was quite unaware of it. Even had she seen the thrush, she would have considered it a signal sign of regard for Miss Dawson on Lord Jim's part for which she should have felt gratitude. Birds, after all,

18

were designed by Nature among their other uses to provide healthy amusement for cats.

Unfortunately the thrush was not an isolated casualty and with each pathetic little corpse, whether laid at her door or found elsewhere, poor Miss Dawson suffered anew and raged inwardly.

2

MISS DAWSON AND MRS PERRY

MISS DAWSON'S room on the second floor was always in a green gloom. Very close to the window were the boughs of the deodar tree. This tree was a perpetual joy to her, not only in itself, its alien mysterious world, the association with a far country of great mountain peaks, but also for its population. Miss Dawson had travelled and bird-watched wherever she went, and photographed and lectured on birds, and her walls were decorated with beautiful prints of rare birds. Seen dimly in the shadowy room, they sometimes seemed alive. But there was no doubt about the busy life that went on among the branches of the deodar. Miss Dawson knew all the tree's regular visitors and residents better than she knew the residents of The Haven, for she was something of a recluse. There were tree creepers, wood pigeons, of course, robins and tits, best of all a pair of gold crests. Miss Dawson was never tired of watching them and listening to their varied conversation. She knew many of the other birds besides, not just the ones that belonged to her tree. The thrush that Lord Jim had brought her had nested for three years past in the old shrubbery lilacs. He had become very tame, which of course was his undoing. Painfully crippled though she was with her arthritis, and only able to walk with sticks, Miss Dawson had managed to wrap up the thrush in a handkerchief and placing it in the bag which she always wore slung round her neck, she edged herself down to Mrs Perry who promised to bury it out of reach of Lord Jim. Not that actually he ever did eat his prey, he was too well fed for that and killed merely for sport.

"I believe you know every bird in this garden," said Mrs Perry to Miss Dawson.

They were having tea together in Mrs Perry's room which had been the morning room. It was one of the lightest and most cheerful in the house, on the south side and with a bow window overlooking her own garden patch. She suffered from a chronic bronchial condition and was always grateful that she had been able to have this particular room. Though she would not admit it, even to herself, Miss Dawson was sometimes quite glad, especially on chilly days when the radiator didn't radiate much, to leave her dim retreat for a time. She had eased herself into the comfortable chair that was always kept free for her and was enjoying the pleasant illusion of an early summer's day provided by the jar of warm coloured wallflowers on the round table and the row of robust polyanthus and primula pot plants on the windowsill. Though a born solitary, she was human enough to feel the need of congenial company sometimes and she had discovered that she and Mrs Perry shared a love of nature, though in somewhat different aspects and ways, for Mrs Perry's feeling for flowers was not in the least professional. They were drawn together, too, by the treatment they had suffered at the paws of Lord Jim.

"It's a wonder there's a bird left for me to know with that wretched cat around," said Miss Dawson.

"He's been taking his usual siesta on the top of my poor pansies," mourned Mrs Perry gently.

"As if birds hadn't enough to put up with," went on Miss Dawson, "with all the destruction of nesting sites that goes on and ghastly pesticides poisoning their food, without cats, and

21

there seems more of them about every year."

"I don't blame Lord Jim so much," said Mrs Perry, "but he is so spoiled. Miss Blackett lets him do just as he likes. She has never attempted to train him."

"You can't train cats," snapped Miss Dawson. "The only thing to do is to get rid of them."

Mrs Perry was silent. She respected her friend too much to contradict her but she knew that you could train cats. Their family cats had all been trained to take "No" for an answer, to keep off flower beds and never to thieve food from tables. She poured herself out another cup of tea.

"I believe Miss Blackett takes the top off all our milk for him," she said, "it's so thin."

"*Most* likely," said Miss Dawson.

"But to do her justice, she probably gives him all the cream off hers first."

"More fool her," said Miss Dawson.

They were interrupted in this comforting talk by Gisela coming in to collect the trays. She seemed upset and nearly dropped a cup. She was easily given to tears and appeared on the brink of them now.

"What's the matter, Gisela?" asked kind Mrs Perry.

"It's that Miss Norton. I do not understand at all. She has beautiful picture of a white horse and many dogs and I try to please and I say: 'Miss Norton, what a beautiful picture of a white horse and many dogs,' and Miss Norton speak quite cross, and she say, 'They are hounds not dogs and the horse, she is grey,' and the horse is white, white, WHITE," her voice went up the scale almost to a shriek, "and I speak English, *not* German and say 'dog' properly and not 'hund'."

It seemed too difficult to try to explain so Mrs Perry merely said, "Never mind, dear, you are getting along very nicely with your English."

Miss Dawson, who took not the slightest interest in Gisela or Miss Norton, simply waited until the room was quiet again.

"Yes, the only way with cats is to get rid of them," she then repeated.

"I can't see how Lord Jim is to be got rid of," said Mrs Perry.

"Where there's a will, there's a way," said Miss Dawson, so firmly that Mrs Perry felt a little disturbed. She wished Frances Dawson had something else to think about than her birds and her tree. She herself had a loving family most of whom, though they were at a distance, regularly phoned or wrote, and there were a couple of nice grandchildren who managed to visit her fairly frequently, and sometimes brought her cuttings and plants, for gardening was a family addiction. She was afraid, too, that Frances was often in pain, she was such a valiant creature that she never complained, and sometimes perhaps it was better to complain a little. She thought she would change the subject.

"The apple blossom's scarcely shown yet, it's been such a cold spring, but the lilac's brave as usual, and the warden was picking a lot of it this morning, for the committee meeting tomorrow, I suppose. It's a funny thing about lilac, sometimes it behaves well when it's picked, but more often than not it wilts in a most tiresome fashion."

"Oh, if there's a committee, I suppose the dining-room will be out of action and we'll have meals in our rooms," said Miss Dawson with some satisfaction.

"Why don't we ask Gisela to bring yours in here and we'll have them together," suggested Mrs Perry.

"No, thank you, Mary," said Miss Dawson. There was a limit to her capacity for companionship and this was reached fairly quickly and often quite suddenly. She was subject, too, to a queer feeling, almost of disloyalty, if she were absent too long from her room and her tree. Mrs Perry did not press her, accepting though not understanding her friend's ways by this

23

time, so that she was sorry but not in the least offended.

The two continued to chat amiably until it was time to prepare for supper. Although the main meal at The Haven was in the middle of the day, the old ladies had been used in past years to changing for dinner and as long as they were able, they did so still. It was part of the courageous losing battle that was perpetually being waged within those discreet walls. Miss Blackett, who shared the midday meal, only "saw to" the supper. She and Lord Jim ate together later when the day's work was almost done and she could relax. It was the favourite hour of her day when, with her television set switched on and Lord Jim purring expectantly at her feet, they could enjoy a snack of whatever took their fancy.

The ladies, in their brave array, a few pieces of jewellery sparkling on old fingers or fastening wraps, sat at an oblong mahogany table in the dining-room. Like them, this table was a relic of a more dignified and prosperous past and made the plastic and steel chairs look like the undeveloped embryos of real furniture. The ladies had to trust themselves to these, however, three on one side and three on the other and one at the end facing the warden.

In the centre of the table was a pot of bright pink hyacinth lolling their top heavy blooms over the edge. Mrs Perry didn't exactly hate them — she couldn't hate any flowers — but she compared them unfavourably with every other spring flower she could think of and their particular shade of pink with every other colour. She herself always grew the more delicate Roman hyacinths that never lolled.

Supper consisted of tomato soup (Heinz), macaroni cheese, not very strongly flavoured and the kind of bread-and-butter pudding that lacked all pleasant surprises. Miss Blackett considered it a good nourishing supper and very suitable for the old. Mrs Thornton, mindful of Nanny, classed it as one of those

24

meals to which she would willingly have summoned as a substitute for herself a starving citizen from the Third World. Miss Dawson did not notice what she was eating, Miss Leila Ford enjoyed it because she loved all food, Mrs Langley smiled happily to herself throughout. Who knows what bygone meal *she* was consuming. Miss Norton, whose sight was very bad, was concentrating too hard on getting the food to her mouth without degrading spillings, to care what it was. Mrs Perry, controlling an itch to tie up those hyacinths properly, thought complacently of a little secret store in her own room which was regularly replenished by thoughtful relatives and friends. She decided that after supper was over she would take some particularly nice shortbread, sent by a niece in Scotland, to cheer up Miss Brown who was eating as little as she dared without attracting Miss Blackett's attention.

The ladies always sat in the same places and when the warden had once tried to change them round, it met with such obvious disapproval that, as it did not really matter at all to her, she gave up the attempt and let the old sillies have their own way. Mrs Thornton, whose seat was between deaf Miss Brown and Mrs Langley, would herself have benefited by a change, but she understood and partly shared in the half-conscious desire for territorial security which, having lost their homes, made each cling to their own place at table and the same chair in the common sitting-room. Conversation at meal times could not be called animated unless the day had brought any unusual visitors or news of any interesting happening from the outside world. Miss Blackett, used in the past to the chattering of noisy small boys, welcomed at first the negative calm of meals at The Haven, but after a while it oppressed her.

"I'll be getting as dumb myself, shut up day after day with the old things," she had complained to Brenda and Gisela one day. She felt it was beneath her dignity to talk in this way to the girls but they hardly noticed. As far as they were concerned, she was already almost in the same category as the old ladies and neither she nor they possessed any real relevance to life.

Supper over, all but Miss Norton, Mrs Thornton and Miss Dawson went into the sitting-room to watch television. As no one was allowed to touch the controls because the warden thought, probably correctly, that this would cause friction, the majority decided on the programmes and she switched them on, very loud and very bright, as she thought this was both necessary and nice. Miss Norton never watched because of her defective sight, Mrs Thornton had her own small set which from her attic fastness she knew could disturb no one. Miss Dawson vehemently disliked all television on principle. This evening, too, she felt very tired but she knew that the pain from her arthritis would only become worse in bed and although allowed two pain killers, doled out to her each evening, she did not allow herself to resort to these so early in the night. She wrapped herself in shawls and a rug and sat in her favourite chair by the window and prayed for the miracle that sometimes some kind magic worked for her. She never knew when it would happen and it was not often, but when it did it was far better than any pain killers. Somehow she thought it might tonight. There was a full moon rising and the softly moving branches of the deodar tree threw shadows on her walls, for she had not switched on her light. The window was slightly open and the distant hoot of an owl floated into the room. Nearer at hand a blackbird was still hard at it and Miss Dawson knew that a thrush or two would follow, singing late into the May night.

The bird's song, though so native, did not seem to conflict with the faint exotic scent from the deodar but mingled subtly with it, creating in Miss Dawson's mind a strange compound of past and present, of scenes near at hand and far away in time and space. Gradually these impressions became more vivid and

26

more compelling. Frances Dawson was now a girl in her father's garden, listening to the promise of summer in the evening bird chorus all about her, excited beyond measure at the mysterious summons of their song. Almost simultaneously she was a much older but a no less happy Frances Dawson. The curtains of her room had changed to the canvas flaps of a tent open to vast distances glimpsed through a fringe of Himalayan pines, standing like huge sentinels round her camping site. She was so high up in the world that she felt almost as free as the bright tropical birds she had been watching all that day. The deep peace of that freedom enveloped her. She turned and stretched luxuriously on her campbed – she nodded and slipped down in her old chair at The Haven and slept deeply and dreamlessly at last. Her miracle had worked once again.

3

MISS NORTON, MISS BROWN, MISS FORD

MISS NORTON negotiated the hall and passage and stairs successfully with the help of her stick which she used for guidance only; she was still erect and agile and needed no prop. She shut the door of her room with relief and triumph. Another day conquered and she could relax completely.

Mrs Thornton, who was the only person likely to visit her, would tonight, as she knew, be listening to a favourite music programme. Since her sight had worsened, each day was a battle to retain her dignity and independence. But she came of fighting stock in which self-pity in misfortune had had little part, though she allowed herself the indulgence of exasperation now and again. For instance, when she realized that she could no longer play her endless games of Patience, that it really was no good (even the largest cards got muddled up), she threw the pack across the room and it took her a long while to locate and retrieve each card. "That'll teach me," she said to herself. But such outbursts were few. In her own room, unless someone had moved any of her things from their accustomed places, she could manage pretty well still and she remained the most immaculately neat, clean and well turned out of all The Haven's residents.

She did not sit down now before she had taken off her beautifully fitting though ancient black velvet gown (definitely a gown and not a mere dress) and hung it carefully in her cupboard. She folded the little muslin scarf she had worn round her shoulders and placed it in her top right-hand drawer among her lavender-scented embroidered handkerchiefs. She took off a pair of elegant pointed shoes and fitted them with their trees, then felt for her slippers beside the bed. They were warm and comforting to her cold feet. Then she put on a loose wrapper and at last seated herself in an upright armchair and switched on her radio to hear the sporting news.

The picture which had caught Gisela's attention dominated the room. It was an oil painting of her father on his favourite hunter with two cavorting foxhounds in the foreground and, behind, a grey stone house of pleasing proportions. Though Miss Norton's eyes could no longer see the picture well, she did not need them to recall its every detail. Beneath it hung two miniatures, one of two children, a boy and a girl, the boy with an arm flung protectively round his sister, for it was easy to see the likeness between the two, though he was dark and straight-haired and she had pale brown curls. It was not difficult either to trace in old Miss Norton the same fine bone structure and the same small head set on a long neck, as in the child's portrait.

The other miniature was of a very fair young man in an army officer's uniform which seemed to eclipse his identity. He looked too young for it. He was indeed, like so many of his contemporaries, too young for what it signified at the time when the picture was painted. Miss Norton had been engaged to him once. He was her twin brother's closest friend and both had passed out of Sandhurst together in the summer of 1914 and had been killed in Flanders in the first battle of Ypres. Her short romance seemed now as if it had happened to someone in a book she had read long ago and when she thought about it, she felt ashamed that she could hardly recall Paul's face or his voice – the miniature had never seemed real. She could only remember

29

how the back of his hands and his arms were covered with fine golden hairs and that he had a habit of softly whistling to himself, whereas she could always still see her brother vividly and hear him speak and laugh.

There was no one else left to marry among the families that her parents knew and "afterwards", as Miss Norton always referred to the years immediately following the War, her parents anyway needed her at home. Her father, always keenly interested in racing, grew reckless. "One must do something, Meg," he had said to his daughter, "you understand, don't you, a man must do something, but promise me you'll never bet yourself." Gradually racing debts piled up and, at his death, the estate and the old house and most of its contents had to be sold. Miss Norton and her mother took a flat in Darnley and there her mother died and, eventually, Meg Norton, whose sight had begun to give serious trouble, moved into The Haven.

She did not make friends there easily. "Stand-offish," said Miss Blackett, but it was really that she had never learned to mix in a wider circle than the narrow one in which she had been reared. She found herself more at ease with Mrs Thornton than the rest. She had been the Squire's daughter in a village and Mrs Thornton's girlhood had been spent in a country parsonage. They had inhabited the same vanished world. It was Mrs Thornton, though, who had made the first overture. She noticed how blind Miss Norton was getting and wondered if she would like the morning papers read to her sometimes. Miss Norton agreed to the suggestion with some hesitation, though grateful for the offer, and Mrs Thornton soon found that she was not much interested. It took several sessions equally boring to both before Miss Norton brought herself to ask for the sports pages. She had kept her promise to her father but retained the interest which she had shared with him. By this time, however, Mrs Thornton had taken note of the row of silver cups on the long

30

shelf opposite the window and was not altogether surprised.

"What a beautiful array you have there, Miss Norton," she said.

"I used to be quite a successful show jumper as a girl," said Miss Norton, "but most of these cups were won by my brother — he was a fine all-round athlete."

Mrs Thornton felt a pang of sympathy and pity, while at the same time she was glad that her shelves held books and not silver cups. She possessed a living heritage from the past and she thought, not for the first time, that old age bore more grievously upon those whose main interests had been in physical activities. So from then on she patiently ploughed through reports of race meetings and when these were exhausted, accounts of cricket, tennis and football events in their due seasons, and followed the careers of notable sportsmen and women of many nationalities for Miss Norton's sake. And then, one day, when she had finished reading about how "Sandhurst Prince won the Sirena Stakes at Kempton Park with consummate ease", Miss Norton surprised her by asking if she knew anything about "Talking Books".

"Indeed I do," said Mrs Thornton. "I have a blind cousin who would not know what to do without them. There is a great variety to choose from, too. Is there any special author you would like me to try and get for you?"

"Do they have any of Shakespeare's plays?" asked Miss Norton. "I am very fond of the plays."

"Now," said Mrs Thornton to herself, "this just shows that nobody really knows anything about anybody when they think they do."

Miss Norton went on, "Of course, I don't understand them properly but you don't need to understand Shakespeare, do you? I mean, not when you have seen him acted. We lived near Stratford, you see, and Harry — that's my brother — was very

31

fond of the theatre. We used to go off together in his holidays, on our bicycles. Coming home at night in the summer it was never really dark. Sometimes there was a bright moon – the honeysuckle smelt so nice in the hedges. It was the old theatre that was burnt down, you know, it had an outside staircase by the river. We used to go down to the river in the intervals – there were no crowds in those days. Then, 'afterwards', I used to go alone. It didn't matter riding home alone at night, then, did it? You might think I wouldn't want to go afterwards, but I did. *Twelfth Night* is my favourite play and then *Henry V*."

So then Mrs Thornton read Shakespeare aloud, too, quite regularly. She tried once or twice to interest Meg in other authors but it was no good. Shakespeare and the sports pages of *The Times* were enough for her. When the plays were being read, Meg Norton would sit perfectly still with her eyes shut and her lips a little parted in rapt attention, as though she were seeing again the long dead actors and actresses playing their various parts.

"She looks like 'Patience on a monument smiling at grief'," thought Mrs Thornton, and then the aptness of the phrase pierced her. "Smiling at grief", "Count your blessings", "Smile at grief". "It ought to be written up over our front door."

But Mrs Perry, seated before the television on the evening when Miss Blackett had picked the lilac and Miss Dawson had experienced her miracle and Mrs Thornton was listening to her music, had really no grief to smile at. She was quite happily knitting a garment for her second great-grandchild and looking up now and again at the Box. She always knitted while she watched. She had been taught as a child that idleness was a sin and though she no longer believed this, the habit of constant employment remained with her. Besides, she liked it, and her knitting was a refuge when the programmes became boring or unpleasant: Mrs Langley did not mind what she watched, she liked the animation of movement and sound and it was for her like the constantly changing kaleidoscope patterns that had delighted her as a child. She nearly always dropped off to sleep after a while. Miss Ford and Miss Brown generally preferred ITV, so ITV it was. Mrs Perry felt ashamed that what she often enjoyed most were the advertisements. Many of them were really clever, she thought, and funny too and the voices that accompanied them, cajoling, menacing, sensational and portentous by turns, never failed to entrance her – they were so ridiculous. She liked it when there were gardening programmes but the best of these were often on the other station and, generally, while supper was in progress, so she missed them. But she liked travel films, too, and some science fiction ones and pleasant family series. What made her concentrate on her knitting was the drearily monotonous sex pictures, always the same with hideous close-ups of people embracing. Really, the human face when blown up to giant proportions was too grotesque. She had read *Gulliver's Travels* once at school and sympathized with Gulliver's disgust at the huge Brobdingnags. The other boring activity was men hitting each other or firing off guns that made her jump and there seemed more of these every week. Still, it all made a change and when she had had enough she gently woke up Mrs Langley and took her safely back to her room before she went to her own. Invariably she left the other two still watching.

Leila Ford, who had been a third-rate actress in her youth, was really only interested in the personalities of the various performers, but Dorothy Brown, whose experience of life had been largely vicarious, lived out each drama, identifying herself, where possible, with the characters and the action so thoroughly that it was a recurring shock to hear Leila's comments. But tonight it was the background rather than the story or actors that gripped her. The scene was set in Greece and for Dorothy this was the land of pure enchantment, where long ago "the light that never was on land or sea" had shone for her once and for all. And, as if it were not enough to be drunk with its beauty, it was in Greece that she had first met Leila, not the monstrously overweight Leila with her bronze wig, now seated beside her in the only really comfortable chair in the room, but a Being in tune with all the magic of the wonderful country around her, a nymph with flowing red-gold hair and a dazzling smile, and outrageously daring clothes and exotic scent unknown in Dorothy's world — and this glorious Being unbelievably had chosen her as a friend and confidante for the rest of that marvellous holiday. The meeting with Leila had shaped the rest of Dorothy's life, whether for better or worse she was not the sort to enquire.

"Look, Leila," she said, "it's Greece!"

"Oh, is it?" said Leila indifferently. "Well, wherever it is, it's not worth looking at any more. That woman is far too old for the part and as for Derek Jones, he's the same boring understudy for Noel Coward whoever he's playing. Let's go to bed."

"Oh, no, Leila," said Dorothy, "do let us stay a bit longer; they might go to Delphi."

Leila turned her head slowly and looked at her. She had singular eyes, large, dark and opaque. "You can stay if you like," she said, "but you know I can't sleep if I don't get off when I feel like it."

Dorothy knew it too well, and she also knew that Leila could not easily undress herself now. She said no more but helped Leila to her feet, as she did so looking her last on all things lovely, the golden glory which the warden would switch off at the regulation time of ten o'clock.

Dorothy Brown was formerly an unsuccessful school teacher. In a modern large comprehensive school she would have been a total failure, but luckily for her when she started her career the times were not yet ripe for this and the girls' school in which she taught was on the whole well mannered and misbehaviour was unobtrusive.

"Oh, heavens! I haven't done my Latin prep. What *shall* I do?"

"Do it in Brownie's geog. lesson; she'll never notice, and if she does, she won't say anything."

Unhappily this was true. Dorothy suspected that her lessons were dull and inefficient, and poor exam results confirmed this, but geography was a second-class subject and so results did not matter all that much and she kept her job, staying on and on because she did not know what else to do until, most unexpectedly, an uncle left her a house and quite a substantial sum besides. Her mother, who had died when Dorothy was a girl, had been his favourite sister but he had lived mostly abroad and she scarcely knew him. She had a stepmother and a father who were not very interested in her, nor did she see any reason why they, or indeed anybody else, should be. She was not particularly able or amusing and, though she had nice grey eyes behind her spectacles, the rest of her appearance was easily forgotten. She could hardly believe in this legacy. She gave in her notice at once and at the end of the next term she left without regrets. Unreasonably, though, she hoped against hope for some sign of regret in others. Two more of the staff were leaving at the same time and they had presents and cards. On the last morning there was actually a card in her pigeon-hole, but it was only a regulation one from the Headmistress – a photograph of the school with "All good wishes for your future" written on it. This somehow made things worse, but travelling home with a wait at a railway junction, her eye was caught by a picture of the Parthenon on a magazine cover. On an impulse she bought it, read an article on "Touring in Greece" and thought wildly, "Why not? I could go there if I wanted to, I, Dorothy Brown, could go to Greece."

She fell in love with Greece when she got there, even before she met Leila. Dorothy was always falling in love with no hope and indeed with no great wish for any return. To be in love was enough. As a girl she had fallen in love with her geography mistress, which was a pity as it led to her taking up a subject in which she had never really been much interested. Then her loves succeeded each other in quick succession. There was Leslie Howard, and Jessie Matthews, and Laurence Olivier, and Vivien Leigh and the young local Conservative candidate who came one day to speak to the school and for whom she afterwards licked many election envelopes, and there was a headgirl, who looked like a fawn and had acted Juliet in the school production so movingly that Dorothy could hardly restrain her tears, and then there was Greece and Leila Ford.

In this, as in much else, Leila was her opposite. Leila had only loved once and for all in her life and was as constant and ardent a lover as any immortalized in literature. She was the only child of a late marriage, but her parents had not wished for any other children who might have deprived their Lilly (for so she had been christened) of their undivided attention. They believed her to be the prettiest and the cleverest little girl in the world, and as soon as she was old enough, which was remarkably soon, she fully agreed with them. Nothing was thought too good for her, but unfortunately this resulted in nothing being quite good enough. As soon as she went to school the trouble began.

"Lilly, teacher says you are to be an angel in the Christmas play."

"But I want to be Mary." And it went on like this.

Lilly really had striking looks but she possessed little real ability and the stage, which had seemed to offer so much glamour as a career, proved hard going. After a few minor engagement with touring companies, she decided marriage was preferable to continuing to cast her pearls before swine. But once again she was dreadfully disappointed.

"Darling," she confided to Dorothy as they gazed together at the columns at Sumnian, "I gave up everything, yes, everything, for him and on our honeymoon I discovered —" she paused and lowered her voice and Dorothy caught her breath in delicious suspense — "I discovered he was a pervert."

Dorothy only had the vaguest idea of what this could mean but obviously it was some almost unmentionable horror, and she thrilled at the thought that this tragic victim, almost in fact an Iphigenia or an Antigone, was actually pouring out her heart to *her*. Yes, the marriage state which should have only brought more gifts to lay at the feet of Leila, the loved one, had had the impudence to demand unpleasant and inexcusable returns. It became obvious to Leila that she must be loyal to her first love — one could not serve two masters.

"It was, of course, impossible to stay with him," she said, "so I went back to my parents, my life ruined."

"Couldn't you have gone on with your acting?" said Dorothy. "You must have been *such* a loss. How I would have loved to have seen you!"

"Darling, the blow was too great, you don't quite understand. Look, we must go, the coach is filling up."

Later, Dorothy learned that it was not long since Leila, who was some years younger than herself, had lost her mother.

"It was her heart. She had just nursed me through influenza and I was away convalescing. She had caught it from me, you see."

"Oh, dear!" said Dorothy. "How you must have suffered not being with her."

"Yes," said Leila, "I was in no state to look after my poor father. He has gone into a very nice Home. I felt I needed a

37

thorough change after all the upset, so I booked this holiday. Darling, you are such a wonderful friend, there is no one here that I could possibly have told of all my troubles."

This was probably true, as Dorothy Brown and herself happened to be the only unattached members of the party, all the rest being married couples or pairs of close friends. In return for such confidences, Dorothy felt that the only item of interest in her own life was her legacy and indeed that seemed to interest Leila greatly.

"And where are you going to live now, dear?" she asked.

"Well, besides the legacy," said Dorothy almost apologetically, "my uncle left me a house in Darnley. I don't suppose you'd have heard of Darnley, it's a little town, really only a large village, in Warwickshire."

"The very heart of old England!" exclaimed Leila.

"But it's really too big a house for me," went on Dorothy, "and my solicitor advises me to sell it, so I may get a flat there instead, or somewhere else I suppose – I don't quite know."

"You vague little thing!" said Leila affectionately.

The day after this conversation, while admiring the stupendous views from Delphi, Leila resumed the subject.

"I think it would be a shame to sell your dear uncle's house. Why not get a friend to share it with you? Two living together is so much cheaper than one."

"I haven't any friend who would want to, I am afraid," said Dorothy. There was silence; the sun was disappearing behind the vast violet mountains and a wild impossible idea invaded her.

"I don't suppose ..." she faltered, "oh, of course not, but you're so kind, you'll forgive me asking, but I don't suppose you could think ever of sharing the house with me yourself."

"You darling thing!" cried Leila. "How marvellous of you to propose such a thing! It might, d'you know, it might be possible, it just possibly might. Let's sleep on it, shall we?"

38

Peacefully Leila slept on it, but Dorothy alternated between huge hopes and fears. She settled for fears, it would be too good to be true. But it wasn't.

In the morning Leila said, "Well, darling, shall we give it a trial?"

When Leila actually saw the house, it obviously wouldn't quite do as it stood, but after getting the willing Dorothy to throw out an extension and put in an extra window to the best room — "After all, dear, it's improving the value of your property" — she found it took in her furniture quite satisfactorily, and so they settled down together and the long years passed, bringing, almost imperceptibly, unhappy changes to both.

For Leila, discontent became a way of life, only assuaged by eating and sleeping; Dorothy, for whom the glory had long departed, was always tired. One day, climbing the hill to Leila's favourite Delicatessen to shop, she had fainted and was brought home in an ambulance. The doctor said she was suffering from severe anaemia. It was just about then that Leila had developed her nervous headaches — she was approaching seventy and Dorothy five or so years older — what was to be done? The answer was found in The Haven where there actually happened to be two rooms vacant at the same time — two adjoining rooms, one large and one small. It was providential.

"How cosy this is," Leila had said, looking round the small one. "You'll be so snug in here, Dot dear."

4

THE COMMITTEE MEETING

MOST COMMITTEES consist of one member (usually the chairman) who appears to be doing a great deal of important work, and another (usually the secretary) who really does it. Besides these two essential components, there is often someone who is constantly puzzled to find themselves on a committee at all, and another who seems to have been born there and whose lifelong hobby is to serve on as many others as possible. Most committees also contain certain ex-officio members of one sort or another and a spare part or two.

The house committee of The Haven was no exception to this. Lady Merivale had a reputation for philanthropy to keep up in her own eyes, as well as among her neighbours, and she was successful as a chairwoman, ordering people about quite naturally and without giving offence. Her secretary, Miss Honor Bredon, was capable, intelligent and hardworking, in fact a good secretary. The treasurer, Colonel Bradshaw (retired) did not do so badly either in what was a somewhat thankless and difficult job, for the finances of the Home were complicated and inadequate and what with inflation and his own kind and conscientious disposition, he spent quite a number of worried hours over The Haven's affairs.

The vicar, an ex-officio member, was more interested in bees than in anything else in this world, or, it must be confessed, in the next. He was secretary to the County Apiary Society and often wished his parishioners were as industrious, clever and orderly as his beloved bees. But he accepted that this was not so, nor ever would be, and he did his duty by them manfully, which included serving on this particular committee and visiting the old ladies from time to time. Miss Hughes, one of the spare parts, possessed a surplus of both money and leisure and too few friends or interests, and so, on looking through her distressingly empty diary, she hailed with delighted the entry for May 10th — "Committee Meeting at The Haven, 2.30 p.m." She had been proposed as a member by Col. Bradshaw at the instigation of his wife, who had refused the honour for herself.

"Yes, I know you are right, Dick, there should be another woman on the committee, considering The Haven is a Home for Old Ladies, but really, what with the Wives' Fellowship and the Conservative Association and the secretaryship of the Bridge Club and the children and the garden, I really can't undertake anything more, and Miss Hughes would love it."

Miss Hughes did love it, only she wished she could think of something important to say at the Meetings. However, she could always assent or dissent heartily to show that she really was deeply involved and interested. Col. Bradshaw cherished a secret hope that one day it might occur to her to donate a small portion of her large income to ease the financial straits of The Haven, but his hope was unlikely to be realized. Her money being her one asset, she naturally clung to it with tenacity. The sixth member of the committee was an architect, a little restless man with a sandy moustache. Someone had once suggested that he could be helpful about problems of conversion and maintenance and might be in touch with cheap or even reasonable contractors. This had not hitherto been so. He spent the time during meetings wondering why he was pointlessly wasting it and drawing little plans and pictures on his agenda paper.

41

Seventh and last was a Mr Martin, the committee enthusiast, passionately addicted to irrelevant detail, but a mine of accurate information which was useful enough to outweigh the irritation he aroused.

Their number happened to be the same as the number of the residents and they sat round the same dignified solid table on the same uncomfortable and far from solid chairs. Only Lady Merivale was provided with an imitation Chippendale, the usual function of which was to lend tone to the entrance hall. The hyacinths, certainly now past their best, had been removed to the sideboard and were replaced by the lilac, picked by the warden the day before, but this had already elected to turn bad-tempered and was lifeless and droopy.

"Flowers always make a place look so homelike," cooed Miss Hughes to Honor Bredon. "Our good Miss Blackett never spares herself, does she, to make everything as pleasant as possible for the old dears."

Honor responded with a little grunt. She found it impossible either to agree or disagree.

Miss Blackett had had a strenuous morning and was looking hot in a too tight flowered artificial silk dress. With only Gisela's inefficient help she had had to prepare the tea which was always provided after the meeting, to see to the dinner trays for the residents, to polish the table and set out the pads and pencils, never used, for members always had their own, but in her eyes the right and proper regalia for any committee. But, as she sank thankfully into her chair, she congratulated herself that all was as it should be and she looked forward to hearing the accustomed expressions of appreciation and confidence which she felt were certainly her due.

The vicar and Col. Bradshaw were discussing the local agricultural show, the architect (who felt the cold) had secured the place nearest to the radiator and was fidgeting about

42

already with paper and pencil, Lady Merivale was condescending pleasantly towards Miss Hughes, when Mr Martin hurried in, having swallowed a hasty sandwich in the train on the way from another meeting. Immediately everyone stopped talking and Lady Merivale picked up her agenda paper and said:

"Well, ladies and gentlemen, I think perhaps we should begin. The first item for discussion, as you will see, is the matter of Mr Jackson's bullocks." Mr Jackson farmed the land adjoining The Haven. "They have apparently broken through the boundary fence and trampled over the copse. Miss Blackett reports that Fred Mills had great difficulty in chasing them back and that their hoof marks are all over the lawn, not to speak of damage done to the fruit trees and the copse."

Col. Bradshaw frowned, Miss Hughes murmured, "Dear, dear, what a pity!", and Mr Martin said: "Madam Chairman, may I ask whose responsibility it is to keep the fence in good repair and could it reasonably be said to be an adequate protection before this invasion?"

Col. Bradshaw said he was afraid the supports of the fence were on The Haven side of the ground, so legally the responsibility for the fence was not the farmer's, but as far as he had ascertained, it was in a fair condition and the bullocks seemed of an exceptionally inquisitive and adventurous breed.

The vicar said he supposed that lot would soon be sold and the trouble wasn't likely to recur. But Mr Martin rustled through his papers, of which he always had a stack, and finding at last the one he wanted, said with some satisfaction:

"Madam Chairman, it appears that this is not an isolated occurrence, in fact it might almost be said to be an annual event. Perhaps Miss Bredon will confirm this?"

Honor, who had already been looking up past Minutes, agreed that earlier bullocks had acted in the same way at least twice before.

Col. Bradshaw admitted that unfortunately Jackson owned a favourite cow, "a fine animal too", who regularly produced a very agile and bold son who was a national leader, and wherever this troublemaker led, the rest of the herd followed.

The architect remarked that this behaviour was not peculiar to bullocks. Mr Martin ignored this irrelevance and asked what should be done to stop the nuisance.

Miss Hughes echoed him with: "What indeed!"

Col. Bradshaw said that what was really needed was electric wiring and Mr Martin said that it was only right that Jackson should contribute to this or sell his cow.

Lady Merivale then proposed that Jackson should be approached by Col. Bradshaw as to the carrying out of some form of effective barrier between his field and the copse. Miss Hughes enthusiastically seconded the motion and the committee moved to the next item, which was the preliminary arrangements for the annual summer fête. The objecte of the fête was threefold – to arouse and maintain local interest in The Haven, to raise a sum of money for "extras" – no really substantial amount could be hoped for – and to give the ladies a chance to contribute articles for sale, so providing them with interest and suitable occupation and the satisfaction of feeling of use.

"Well, Miss Blackett," said Lady Merivale, "who can we count on among our flock?"

"Mrs Perry will have some pot plants ready, I am sure, though I feel bound to say that she is not always prepared to give of her best."

"She regards them as her children," explained the vicar, "and finds it hard to part with any of them, but she is a charming old lady, and when it comes to the point, she'll be generous, I'm sure, and all her plants are well worth buying."

Miss Hughes, who had never set eyes on Mrs Perry or her

44

plants, assented heartily.

Miss Blackett sniffed a little resentfully and continued: "Mrs Thornton is making some quite pretty little patchwork cushion covers."

"Now, I've always longed to do patchwork," said Miss Hughes.

"Miss Norton is too blind to produce anything herself, but she has written to a nephew who has just returned from service abroad and she is sure he will send us some attractive foreign articles."

"Splendid," said Lady Merivale.

"Miss Ford is knitting squares which Miss Brown will make up into a coverlet," continued Miss Blackett. Knitting squares was always a last resort for the least capable of the ladies.

"And they can be very pretty and useful," said Lady Merivale, "I see that as usual you have home supplies well in hand, Miss Blackett. Colonel Bradshaw, I hope Mrs Bradshaw will undertake the produce stall as usual?"

"Yes, I think you may count on her. Oh, she did ask me to mention that she hoped her stall could be sited in the shade this year. Last summer she said all the shady positions were taken before she could get here and the Produce Stall she feels, by its nature, should have priority. Her goods really did suffer rather badly," he added apologetically.

"Oh, what a pity!" exclaimed Miss Hughes.

Honor Bredon made a note to see what could be done, but the question of sites was a tricky one.

"Madam Chairman," said Mr Martin, "I believe it is the custom for the committee to provide the raffle prizes and that these are promised well in advance."

"I'll send along a bottle of sherry," said Col. Bradshaw.

"A pot of honey from me," said the vicar. "My white clover is a general favourite."

Mr Martin said he knew of a firm that would let him have fancy notepaper at a wholesale price, Lady Merivale always gave a large box of chocolates and the architect, with a decent show of diffidence, promised a framed drawing of the Old Market Cross done by himself.

Col. Bradshaw then looked encouragingly at Miss Hughes, who was reviewing in her mind the contents of her gift drawer. It contained, as far as she could remember, an orange silk lampshade and a set of plastic ashtrays, pink, blue and green, a pink satin nightdress case, a stuffed fashion doll bearing a faint likeness to Marilyn Monroe, a large tartan pincushion, a handbag in the shape of a rabbit with artificial fur and glass eyes, and a smart looking stainless-steel (but thoroughly unreliable) clock. All these articles had been bought as bargains or as the cheap left-overs from Bring-and-Buys, and were useful for the birthdays of her domestic 'helps' or for occasions like the present one. She decided on the clock as her raffle contribution, it really did look very well.

The next matter was not disposed of so easily − it had to be decided every year: should there be a band? The Boys' Brigade was available but it was quite expensive and consumed a good deal of refreshments besides. On the other hand, a band always attracted people. But then should there be a marquee in case of rain? They could not afford both. As it was a chilly afternoon, the committee were quite illogically inclined to be gloomy about future weather prospects; rain seemed more likely than not and rain without a marquee would be disastrous, so the marquee won the day. Miss Blackett felt relieved; she hated uncertainty and the strain of watching the weather. It was decided to appoint a small sub-committee nearer the date to help with all the other arrangements.

The afternoon was slipping by and Lady Merivale brought the business of the fête to an end and passed on to the next item, which was to record the vacancy left by the departure of Mrs Wilson for the local hospital where most of the old ladies ended their days when they had passed beyond the care of The Haven. The next name on the waiting list was a Mrs Nicholson who was unable, owing to heart trouble, to continue to run her own home. Miss Blackett felt that the time had now come for a protest and an appeal.

"Lady Merivale," she said, "I am sorry to say that Brenda Jones, my only domestic help beside Gisela, the German au pair, and Mrs Mills who, as you know, only comes to me twice a week, has left me without notice. This Mrs Nicholson does not sound as though she will be able to do much for herself and I feel I cannot undertake this fresh responsibility and the extra work a new resident entails under present conditions. Then Mrs Langley's condition has deteriorated during the past year and she needs constant supervision. I feel she should receive better attention than I can give her, certainly now without Brenda, and I think she should be removed to the geriatric department at the hospital as soon as they have a bed free."

There was a general murmur of sympathy and assent.

"Of course, Miss Blackett," said Lady Merivale, "we cannot let you be overworked and it does seem as though Mrs Langley is not a case for The Haven any more. Will you get Dr Moss to see her and then I am sure he will be able to arrange matters for you."

But the vicar looked uneasy. His visits to the geriatric unit were not among his happiest.

"Mrs Langley is very contented here," he said, "it will be a great change for her. No doubt she will get every physical care at the unit but has she not any relatives who might give her a home? I believe there is no lack of means to provide help and considering her age, it cannot be for very long."

"She has a son close on seventy – the last time he visited her, which was some years ago as he is not in good health, she could not be persuaded that he was not her father. There is a married daughter in Canada and one grandson, a businessman in Birmingham," said Miss Blackett.

"I presume he or his father have powers of attorney," said Mr Martin. "They should be informed of the position."

Honor made another note.

Miss Blackett felt she had done well so far and continued firmly: "If Mrs Langley goes there will be another room vacant. I don't think I can cope with two new residents at once and besides I think it would be far better for Mrs Thornton to move down from the attic floor which is really not suitable for an old person and it would ease the work considerably."

"Quite, quite," said Miss Hughes, but as no one else spoke she felt she had been too precipitate.

"It has always been the custom, as I am sure you know, Miss Blackett," said Lady Merivale after a short pause, "to allow residents their choice of rooms whenever possible but I quite see your point and, if Mrs Thornton agrees, there perhaps should not be any objection."

"It will reduce our income," said Col. Bradshaw.

"Do you know what Mrs Thornton thinks about it?" asked the vicar.

Miss Blackett was an honest woman. She knew that Mrs Thornton had reacted unfavourably to the hints she had thrown out up to the present, but she also believed her to be a sensible person at heart, in other words that she would come to see things as she, Miss Blackett, saw them, so she replied with conviction that though the old always took a little time to adjust to any change, she was sure Mrs Thornton would welcome it quite soon.

"I think then we should wait for the decision to come from her," said the vicar firmly. Mrs Thornton was a clergyman's daughter.

"But, Madam Chairman," said Mr Martin, "if our warden has insufficient help for too many duties, all the residents will suffer. I suggest that we advertise for help at once in the local papers and explore every avenue."

Miss Blackett knew too well all those dead-end avenues but she merely said a little tartly, "The papers are already full of such advertisements."

The vicar cleared his throat and this time spoke with some hesitation.

"I do happen to know of a lad who is quite handy and very willing and is anxious to find work. If you would consider him, Miss Blackett, merely as a stopgap, you know, until you can find someone more suitable, and take him on trial, it might 'bless she who gives and he who takes'," he finished with a nervous flourish.

"Beggars can't be choosers," said Miss Blackett ungraciously, "but I must say I wouldn't choose a boy. What sort of a boy is he?"

"Well, you may not think the sex the only disadvantage," said the vicar hesitantly and paused.

"Come, come, out with it, Vicar," said Mr Martin. "He isn't a Borstal boy on probation, I hope?"

"Oh, no, no, nothing of that sort," said the vicar hastily, "but he's a simple fellow, definitely E.S.N., so his school says, but they speak quite highly of his character and I have been employing him a little on odd jobs and find him an attractive lad, though a bit odd – he has a wonderful way with bees."

"But I don't keep bees," said Miss Blackett.

"No, no, of course not," said the vicar sadly.

"If he's E.S.N. he can't expect much in the way of wages," said Col. Bradshaw.

"Where does he come from?" asked the architect.

49

"He has been living with his grandmother, old Mrs Hobb at Sturton," said the vicar. Sturton was the hamlet about three miles from The Haven. "But she is anxious for him to learn to be independent of her though she seems very fond of him. She wouldn't expect anything but pocket money and his keep."

"Hobb, did you say?" said Col. Bradshaw. "Family's been in these parts since the Conquest I should think but nearly all gone now. The old woman is quite a character, I've heard."

Miss Blackett was silent. The boy sounded very unreliable but she thought of piles of dirty dishes, of unswept floors, of beds to be made, trays to be set and carried about, vegetables to be prepared and all the cooking and the shopping and the fête ahead, not to speak of the possible crises that were apt to occur at any time, and so at last she said: "Well, I'm used to looking after old loonies, so I suppose I can take a young one on, and if the vicar can assure me that he is honest and clean, I dare say he'll be better than nobody."

The committee were relieved at her decision, though not for the first time deploring the warden's way of expressing herself, but still, so they told themselves, her bark was worse than her bite.

"I'm sure you won't regret it," said the vicar. "When can I send him round to see you?"

"Tomorrow evening," said Miss Blackett.

"The next item," said Lady Merivale, "and one that Miss Blackett feels is urgent to put in hand before next autumn, is the felling of the deodar tree."

"It's a fine tree," said Col. Bradshaw. "Must be over a hundred years old."

"It is far too near the house," said the little architect. "People will make that mistake in planting trees. They seem unable to grasp the fact that trees grow and houses can't run away from them."

50

Miss Blackett looked gratified at this support.

"That is exactly the case here," she said. "The tree makes poor Mrs Dawson's room very dark and cheerless and in wet weather the rain collects on the branches which brush against the walls. I feel sure this causes damp."

"Then there seems a strong case for the felling," said Mr Martin.

"It's a fine tree," repeated the colonel sadly, "and it will cost a good deal to fell, though the timber ought to fetch something."

The architect was asked if he knew of any reasonable and trustworthy tree doctors, but it was Mr Martin, of course, who was able to supply names and addresses. The matter of repairs and repainting was soon dealt with and at last the meeting was over. The warden went to help Gisela bring in the tea. The architect and Mr Martin both swallowed a hasty cup and disappeared. Col. Bradshaw, after disposing of one of Miss Blackett's uninteresting little cakes, asked Honor Bredon to come and inspect the damage done by the bullocks. Lady Merivale was left with Miss Hughes. Lord Jim, who had been sulking at having been shut out of the dining-room all the afternoon, had bolted in as soon as the door was opened and after taking a look from the window to make sure that nothing of note was happening in the drive, made straight for Miss Hughes, who disliked all animals but perhaps more especially cats. He wrapped himself ecstatically round her ankles. She exclaimed, stepped back hurriedly and jerked Lady Merivale into upsetting her cup of tea down her pale grey linen suit. Miss Hughes apologized effusively, Lady Merivale said it really didn't matter in the least, and Lord Jim went to the door which someone had closed again and demanded to be let out immediately.

"A very useful meeting, don't you think, Miss Hughes?" said Lady Merivale pleasantly.

51

"Oh, yes, very!" agreed Miss Hughes.

"I wonder if you could spare some of your valuable time to help with the fête," went on Lady Merivale, "perhaps as a stall-holder?"

"I think I could manage it," said Miss Hughes delightedly.

"That would be most kind," said Lady Merivale drawing on her gloves. "Well, I think I must be off now, Miss Blackett. Thank you as usual for all your splendid work for us and for your hospitality this afternoon. I am sure you have decided rightly in giving this poor boy a trial and I do hope he will prove a real help to you."

"I hope so too," replied Miss Blackett, but the hope was faint. Life had not taught her to be very hopeful.

5

TOM

The vicar often liked to go about his business on his push bicycle. He said it was good for him and besides, it left the car free for his wife. She was the better driver and by far the better mechanic of the two. On the morning after the committee meeting, he set out to visit Tom Hobb and his grandmother. The weather at last had taken a turn for the better. The east wind which had blown relentlessly since early April had veered to the south-west and everything beautiful could stop looking brave as well and instead rejoice in shining with a quite remarkable loveliness. The vicar sped along the road leading to the hamlet and as he passed The Haven he waved courteously to the house, thinking that one of the old ladies might chance to be looking out of a window and be cheered at the gesture. Soon he turned into a lane bordered thickly with cow parsley, the hawthorn was out in the hedges and there were great clumps of campion on the banks and here and there a single foxglove reared up like a sentinel. A few white clouds were rapidly disintegrating in a sky of deep secure blue and the sun felt really hot for the first time that year.

The vicar could not contain himself. "Praise God from Whom all blessings flow," he roared out and flew down the lane at a dangerous speed. He was a man given to happiness. He had his bees, a wife who was admirably fitted to be a vicar's helpmate, two pretty small daughters and an uncomplicated mind. Of course he was sometimes troubled about erring or sorrowful parishioners, and he made himself miserable for a short time once a day by reading or listening to the news. But this he felt was enough. His wants were few and he had no ambitions to speak of, so on this fine May morning he sang the Doxology as he sped through the sunshine.

Tom Hobb's grandmother lived at the bottom of a steep, rough little footpath leading off the lane that continued on its way to the hamlet. The vicar proceeded down this path on foot. The Hobbs' cottage was tiny, humped and thatched, and sat square across the path with a lilac bush and an old apple tree, both in flower, on either side of the gate. On the crest of the thatch, which was in need of repair, crouched a black cat watching the sparrows and in the cottage doorway sat old Mrs Hobb stirring something in a basin. She was noted in the hamlet for her herb potions and her homemade wines and was held to be very ancient and crafty. "A hundred years or so ago she would certainly have been the village witch," thought the vicar, as he propped his bicycle against the hedge, and indeed she looked the part, with her black cat and her pot. The village children were a bit frightened of her, though they all liked Tom. She had had a husband once, it was supposed, and children and other grandchildren, but Tom now seemed to be the only one left. He had always lived with his grandmother and no one could remember his parents being around.

"Good morning, Mrs Hobb," shouted the vicar, coming up the path, "what a lovely day at last."

"And so it be, sir," said the old woman looking up at him with eyes surprisingly bright in a face as brown and crumpled as a winter leaf. "And what can I do for you today?"

It was, as a greeting, the other way round from those he was used to, and took him a little aback.

"Well, it's about Tom. He's been helping me with my bee

54

swarms after school, you know, and now he's finished his schooling, he tells me you'd like him to find a regular job away from home, but not too far away, and I think I've found just the place for him." He paused, she had not taken her eyes from his face and now she nodded vigorously.

"T'would be best for the lad to see a little more of the world," she said.

"I'm afraid you may miss him and the help he is to you," said the vicar. He had thought of this before and wondered if the old woman would be all right on her own, but her gaze did not falter.

"I can manage, sir, and if you have somewhere in mind that is not too far, perhaps he can come and see me of a Sunday."

"It's at The Haven," said the vicar. "Miss Blackett, who is warden there, needs help now, though it may be only temporary."

"The Haven," said the old woman slowly, "that's what they calls the New House that was raised where the Old Farmhouse stood."

"Well, it's scarcely new now," said the vicar smiling.

"Why, no to be sure, but my Mammy, she allays called it the Old Farm when she were a slip of a girl. She'd be pleased for Tom to go there, I expect, even though it is the New House now."

"Miss Blackett wants to see him first," said the vicar, and felt bound to add: "Of course, she may not think him suitable."

"My Tom will suit all right, there'll be no need to be wary of him – there's more corn than chaff in Tom," said the old woman quietly.

"She's as proud of him as if he had left school top of the class instead of not knowing how to read or write and only counting on his fingers," thought the vicar, but aloud he said: "I know he's a good boy and will do his best. Miss Blackett would like to see him this evening. Where is he, by the way? I'd better have a

55

word with him if I can."

"He be gone to gather a bit o' fire wood, sir, and I can't say exactly when he'll be home again." Then, "Ah yes, but I can," she added smiling, for the black cat had suddenly leapt to the ground and streaked round the corner of the cottage. "Sweep allays knows afore I do. Tom'll be here in a moment, you'll see."

Sure enough, the boy came up almost at once with Sweep on his shoulders and a bundle of wood under one arm. He was small for his age but with a big head, and his large ears standing out from it made it look even bigger. His arms seemed too long for his body. His hair was straw-coloured, coarse and thick, he had a snub nose, freckles, greenish eyes set wide apart and a large cheerful mouth. Those eyes did not appear at all vacant, yet there was something not quite usual in the way they looked at you: they turned the same intent disinterested gaze on everything alike. It always reminded the vicar of the way babies he christened gazed at him – if they were not yelling, that is.

"What sort of wood have 'ee got there, then?" asked the old woman.

"A bit o'beech, Granny," said Tom. His voice was pleasantly pitched and he talked like his grandmother and not as they had tried to teach him at school.

The old woman looked pleased. "Good boy, I thought you'd have more sense than to bring any of they dead elm branches from yonder. Burning elm's no better than burning churchyard mould for the warmth."

The boy put down the bundle he was carrying without haste and held out his hand, which the vicar took and solemnly shook. He was, by now, used to Tom's ways.

"Well, Tom," he said, "I think I've found a good place for you and your Granny's willing for you to try it. You're to go and see about it this very evening."

"Where be it then?" asked Tom.

"It's at the Darnley Ladies' Home."

The boy looked puzzled. "There's many a lady's home at Darnley," he said, "there's Jenny's mother's, and Mary's, and Tim's and old Mrs Martin's and —"

"No, no," said the vicar, "not that kind of home, Tom, but a big house called 'The Haven', you must know it well — it stands by itself a little way out of town. A number of old ladies live there together — it's rather like one of my beehives, Tom," he went on, warming to his exposition. "They each have a room to themselves like a cell and there's one lady who looks after them all. Her name is Miss Blackett and you must ask for her when you go there."

"Be she like the queen bee, then?" asked Tom.

"Well, yes, something like that," said the vicar. "You are to go and see her at six o'clock and I've told her you are a very good boy and will do your best to help her."

"Aye, that he will," said the old woman. Tom nodded and held out his hand again as there seemed to him there was nothing more to be said on the subject.

Mrs Hobb got up stiffly to bid the vicar goodbye. She thanked him for coming but it was clear from her manner that she felt she was conferring a benefit and not receiving one. The vicar thought: "I hope she *will* be able to manage without the boy, but it's clear she's made up her mind to part with him and nothing will budge her. Well, anyway, his keep will be a saving for her. I hope, too, he'll make good at The Haven."

"You'll let me know how things go," he said to them both. "It'll be easier to start now summer's really come. We've waited long enough for it this year and it was a hard winter, too."

"Oh, well," said the old woman, "we've never died of a winter yet."

Tom presented himself at the correct hour that evening. He wore a clean darned pullover with sleeves that were too short for

57

his long arms and his trousers were patched. His hair looked very bristly and he was smaller and more childish looking than Miss Blackett had expected, so altogether he did not make a favourable first impression when Gisela had pushed him disdainfully through the office door. The warden did not think it necessary to get up to receive him but Tom came forward at once and held out his hand in his usual way saying:

"Be you Queen Miss Blackett, lady?"

Miss Blackett mechanically shook his hand but was struck dumb by this unlooked-for greeting. She had expected some stupidity perhaps, certainly shyness and even becoming awe. Tom waited for her to speak and looked round him with his wide detached stare. He saw Lord Jim, asleep on his special cushion and immediately went up to him.

"Don't touch him," said Miss Blackett, "he doesn't like to be disturbed, especially by strangers." But neither Tom nor Lord Jim took any notice of her words. Tom stooped and stroked him and the big cat opened his eyes, rolled over on his back and began to purr loudly.

"What be his name?" asked Tom.

"Lord Jim," said Miss Blackett, once more taken aback. Tom nodded his head in approval. Lords, he knew, were very fine people and this was a very fine cat.

"He's bigger nor our Sweep. Do 'ee know why we calls him Sweep? It was one day, Gran and I be sitting by our fire and right through our window he came a-leaping, and across the room and up the chimney afore we could stop him. Gran says a fox must a bin after him. We got a pail o' water quick and threw it on the fire, so as it wouldn't burn him, and after a long while down he comes and all the soot with him. We never found out where he comes from and he's bin with us ever since. So we called him Sweep — it's a good name 'cause he's black as soot anyways."

"This must stop," thought Miss Blackett; the interview (which could scarcely yet have been called an interview) was getting out of hand and she decided to ignore all that Tom had said or done since he had come into the room.

"You're small for your age," she said disapprovingly. "I hope you'll be able to manage what I shall need you to do, if I decide whether to give you a trial. I shall want you to rake out the boiler and stoke it every morning and evening and fill the fuel pails and keep the boiler room clean."

Tom nodded.

"And you must sweep the stairs every day and help Gisela to carry the trays up and down and clean the ladies' rooms."

Tom nodded again.

"Well," said Miss Blackett, "we shall see. I am willing to try you because the vicar says you are a good, hard-working boy, but you must prove to me to be so here as he tells me you have been to him at the vicarage."

"Yes, Queen, Lady Miss Blackett," said Tom and he held out his hand again.

"You mustn't be a silly boy," said Miss Blackett and this time, being more prepared, she took no notice of his hand but continued: "And you must call me Miss Blackett and nothing else." What could have made him bestow royalty upon her? Nevertheless, a faint absurd flicker of gratification stirred within her. He had spoken in such a natural sort of way, not at all impertinently, though what he said was so ridiculous, and yet he was not exactly polite either. She could not describe it.

"Be I to come tomorrow then?"

Miss Blackett considered. She did not like doing anything in too much of a hurry, but if the boy was to come at all, there seemed no point in putting it off. "You can come tomorrow afternoon," she said.

After he had gone she sat for a while thinking. "I don't know

59

quite what to make of him," she said to herself, "and I doubt if he'll be of much use. Oh, well, I didn't hope for much after all. I'll just have to see."

Tom was to sleep in the little attic next to Mrs Thornton. To say that the warden had planned this with a view to reducing Mrs Thornton's contentment with her room would be untrue, for there was no other place to put the boy. Brenda had shared a room with Gisela. But it certainly crossed her mind. She was sure that Mrs Thornton would see reason eventually but it would be all to the good if the process could be speeded up, and she thought it likely that Mrs Thornton would not welcome Tom's advent, banging his door morning and night, as likely as not, and probably making his presence felt in other undesirable ways. She went up to the attic floor the next morning to inspect the little room and to tell Mrs Thornton about the boy.

The small attic had retained more of its original appearance than any other part of the house. It still contained the iron bedstead which had been used by the last of the family cooks, and hanging above it was a framed text – "Thou, God, seest me", illustrated by a huge eye whose black lashes rayed out like beams from a dark sun. There was a scratched deal chest of drawers painted green. Miss Blackett pulled out the drawers, which stuck badly. They were quite empty except for a black-headed hatpin. There was a high bent-wood chair of the kind that used once to be found at every shop counter and a corner washstand, also painted green, holding a chipped white basin and jug. The floor was bare except for a rag rug by the bed. These were all original furnishings but piled along one end of the room were a number of incongruous articles put there to be out of the way – a dressmaker's dummy topped with a torn red silk lampshade, an old knife-cleaning machine, a pile of bound copies of *Sunday at Home* and an umbrella.

Miss Blackett decided that Tom's first job would be to clean

the room. She had no intention of doing it for him – he was
coming to reduce work, not to add to it. She must look out some
bedding for him, however. As for the junk, it would have to stay
there. She did not think it would do for jumble even and the
dustmen were very choosey about what they consented to take
away. If only people wouldn't collect so many articles round
themselves; the old ladies' rooms were a constant source of
irritation to her, cluttered up as they nearly all were, and
everything having to be dealt with somehow when the poor old
things died, and meanwhile having to be kept clean. She always
returned to her own sparsely furnished quarters with a sense of
relief. There was Mrs Thornton's room, for instance, smothered
in books, and books of all things attracted dust. She knocked at
the door.

Mrs Thornton was sitting by the window in her turret
watching for the mid-morning train. She liked to see it
punctually on its way.

"Oh, Mrs Thornton," said Miss Blackett, "there is a boy,
recommended by the vicar, coming to help till we can fill
Brenda's place more adequately. He's to sleep in the little attic. I
hope he won't be a nuisance to you."

"She doesn't really hope anything of the sort," thought Mrs
Thornton, well aware by now of the warden's wish to move her
downstairs.

"I certainly hope not, Miss Blackett," she said coldly.

There was a slight pause and then Miss Blackett went on: "I
am sure there is nothing to worry about, but I think perhaps you
should know that, though a nice enough boy – he came to see
me yesterday – and highly spoken of by both his school and the
vicar, he is rather simple." She would have preferred not to
mention this and to have let Mrs Thornton discover Tom's
deficiencies for herself, but although she was convinced that he
was harmless, he certainly was odd and her conscience told her

it was only fair to warn Mrs Thornton of this. Miss Blackett was in the habit of obeying her conscience.

Mrs Thornton grew more and more indignant and apprehensive as she listened. "This is really too bad," she thought, "not only a boy, but a mentally defective boy on my doorstep. I shan't pretend not to mind." She didn't.

"I was afraid you might not like it," said Miss Blackett, "but it really can't be helped. I am sure you see that he is needed and there is nowhere else to put him. When Mrs Langley goes you can always move down there, you know, such a nice room."

She turned and walked briskly away.

"Oh, indeed I can, can I?" said Mrs Thornton grimly, not caring whether she was heard or not. She recognized that the warden had reason on her side but over this she herself could not be reasonable. She looked round her room with something like desperation: its charms and its privacy seemed all the more precious now that they were threatened. She thought of her lost home with a fierce nostalgia. Her attic represented the last little bit of personal choice left to her and she was determined not to be driven out of it by all the demented boys in Christendom.

Gisela had been crying again. Her letter from home was overdue and still hadn't come that morning. When she brought in Miss Blackett's eleven o'clock coffee she was sniffing.

"If you've caught a cold, it's your own fault, Gisela," said Miss Blackett. "In all this cold weather we've been having, you've been going about in short-sleeved flimsy dresses. We have a very sensible old English saying: 'Ne'er cast a clout till May be out.' That means, don't leave off your warm clothes till the end of the month. Some people think it refers to the blossom May, but I am sure the month is meant. The boy, Tom Hobb, is coming this afternoon. I want you to take him up to his room and tell him to give it a good sweep out. You must show him where everything is kept."

Gisela now felt aggrieved as well as unhappy. She hadn't got a cold and her clothes were the right ones for the time of the year — it was a stupid saying, that! It didn't even know what it meant, if people had to guess at it — and she resented having to bother with a rough boy. She had not at all liked his clothes or his clumsy looks, so that when Tom arrived she would not shake hands but marched on ahead of him ordering him to follow her. Tom was carrying a small bundle.

"What's that for luggage!" said Gisela disdainfully as they reached the attic and he put it down. He was looking at her with his unblinking direct gaze. "Why do you look at me so, it is not good," she said.

"You be so pretty," said Tom.

Gisela knew she was not pretty. She was, in fact, used to being called the plain one of the family. She was tall and thin with straight string-like fair hair. She was too pale, even her eyes were too pale a blue and her nose was long and a little crooked.

"Like one o' they moon daisies," said Tom.

Gisela, in her turn, gazed at him. Just as Miss Blackett had done, she sensed at once that he was not being rude and she began to stop feeling cross and smiled at him unwillingly, for it was rather nice to be called pretty for once, even though it was only by a rough poor boy, and then something in the way his yellow hair stood up like a brush reminded her of her youngest brother, the one she liked the best.

"Come," she said, "you like that I help you with the room?"

Tom nodded and looked round the attic. When he saw the dummy with the lampshade hat, he pointed at it and crowed with laughter. Gisela laughed too and suddenly she felt happy. Even if he was a peasant boy, he was young and, since Brenda had left, she had felt so lonely among all the ladies and Miss Blackett and Mrs Mills and Fred — all so old.

They set to work together moving everything out on to the

63

landing so that they could clean and sweep properly. They pushed open the window, stiff with years of neglect, and Tom stuck his head out and crowed again with pleasure.

"I've never slept so near the sky afore," he said.

Mrs Thornton had heard all the noise and laughter with dismay. It was going to be just as bad as she had feared. She was too upset to tell herself that it was unreasonable to pass judgement so soon. In this mood she spent the rest of the afternoon and most of the evening, waiting for every fresh sound, until at last she realized she must take herself in hand, so she found her *Radio Times* and turned the pages anxiously. Yes, she was in luck, and soon the divine melody of Beethoven's Violin Concerto flooded the room, routing for the time being the world, the flesh and the devil.

At the end of the first movement she heard a slight scuffling noise outside the room and quickly opened the door. Someone, crouched against it outside, nearly fell in. It was a boy – *the* boy, she supposed. She switched off the radio and demanded angrily what he was doing there. Tom replied by humming, in time and in tune, the concerto's opening theme. Mrs Thornton stared down at him and he hummed the tune again and then, pointing beyond her into the room he said:

"Can you play a bit more o' that, Lady, please?"

Mrs Thornton was amazed. She said, "So you were listening to the music, were you? Have you ever heard that piece before?"

Tom shook his head vigorously.

"And you liked it, I can see. Do you like music?" Tom nodded as vigorously.

Mrs Thornton experienced a blessed sense of relief. She could put up with much from a boy who could hum a Beethoven theme correctly after a first hearing, and there was something else as well as relief. The boy obviously really loved what he had

64

heard. She was as convinced of that as Miss Blackett and Gisela had been of his admiration of them. There was no one at all at The Haven besides herself to whom music mattered. Mrs Perry enjoyed Gilbert & Sullivan and Strauss waltzes from early associations, Mrs Langley loved hymn tunes, and Gisela sometimes strummed "Ach du liebe Augustin" on the old piano in the sitting-room, but that was as far as it went, and now this boy, whose invasion on her attic floor she had so resented, was apparently a comrade in felicity. She felt profoundly grateful that, even in old age, life offered such surprises.

6

TOM AND THE LADIES

TOM'S PECULIAR crow of laughter became a familiar sound at
The Haven during the weeks that followed. To Gisela it brought
a sense of fellow feeling and made her giggle. Mrs Thornton, too,
liked to hear it. She became thoroughly interested in Tom and
quite often of an evening she would invite him into her room to
share a radio concert with him. She found that he was always
affected by the music, but that she could not tell beforehand how
he would react. Sometimes he could not remain still but jumped
about in a queer clumsy dance, or clapped his hands and nodded
his head to the rhythm; sometimes he sat motionless as if
enchanted, sometimes he rocked to and fro with laughter and
sometimes he put his fingers to his ears and rushed away out of
the room. She made an attempt to teach him to play on the
sitting-room piano, but, though he could pick up quite
complicated tunes very quickly and hum them correctly, the
mysteries of the keyboard were obviously beyond him, or else he
simply wasn't interested.

Old Mrs Langley was always especially kind to Tom because
she got it into her head that he was her Susan's love-child. "He
always was happy from a baby," she told everyone.

Mrs Perry said it was good to hear him laughing about the
house, it reminded her of her grandchildren. Dorothy Brown
only heard it faintly.

"You grow deafer every day," said Leila, aggrieved. Leila hated Tom. "I never could bear defectives," she said, "and that noise he makes gives me the creeps. I'm a very sensitive person, I'm afraid, but I don't think it's fair to employ a boy like that here. I shall complain."

As for Miss Blackett, she found the laughter disquieting, she did not know why, but it was part of her uncomfortable inability to place Tom in her scheme of things. She could not make him out and this annoyed her. At the end of the first week she had decided to keep him on for there was no doubt he was a good little worker, thorough and willing and much quicker and neater than she had expected from his looks. But he had odd habits. For one thing, as the summer advanced, he seemed to wake earlier and earlier and would come down and set about his work before anyone else was astir. At first she determined to put a stop to this, not that anyone complained, for he was a surprisingly quiet worker and the offices in the annexe were shut off from the rest of the house. But it was not what she was used to.

"You must not come downstairs so early, Tom," she told him, "there is no need — there is plenty of time for you to do your work later."

But the day after she had spoken and all the mornings that followed, it was just the same. She expostulated but she might as well have not spoken. It was most irritating, yet there was no denying that after all it was pleasant to find everything swept and tidy when she herself got downstairs, and the boiler fire giving no trouble, and the breakfast trays set out for Gisela, who on the other hand was apt to be late, and Miss Blackett often had had to see to these herself. And there were little extra jobs done without the asking, such as Lord Jim's breakfast Whiskas tin opened and his evening snack plate cleared up, and the kettle on for her early cup of tea. But then, there was the affair of the bats. A pair of them had taken up daylight residence in a corner of Tom's attic and Miss Blackett, who looked upon bats as vermin, told Tom to get the kitchen steps and get rid of them, but Tom had said, "Best let 'em bide and have their sleep out, Lady Miss Blackett," and when she went up the next day to inspect, they were still there. She had a horror of the creatures and could not bring herself to go near them, but she was unwilling to confess this or to own up to the fact that apparently she was powerless to get Tom to do as he was told – so the bats remained.

His disregard of her orders in certain matters, though never rude or defiant, naturally upset her and it did not happen only to her. Fred Mills, the old gardener, complained that Tom picked flowers from the garden occasionally without asking leave, and Mrs Perry, with some unwillingness, confirmed this.

"I've told the lad they're not his flowers and he's no right to them," grumbled Fred, yet Tom continued to make up his little nosegays quite openly.

What he did with them Mrs Perry later discovered when one day she noticed Miss Brown with a bunch of her treasured clove-pinks pinned to her flat chest.

"What lovely flowers," Mrs Perry shouted pleasantly.

Miss Brown actually blushed. "Tom brought them to me," she said. "He brings me flowers now and again, and I like to wear some of them sometimes, just to show how I appreciate them."

Mrs Perry, who had always felt a little sorry for Miss Brown, said no more. "She obviously doesn't wonder where he gets them from. Poor thing, I wonder if anyone's ever bothered to give her flowers before," she thought.

As for old Fred, he was completely won over by what happened when, before the repairs to the fence had been completed, Mr Jackson's bullocks staged another marauding expedition. This time, however, Tom was on the scene. "I never seed the like. That lad just told 'em to go home, just went up to that little devil of a leader, he did, and stood right in his way and put out his hand to him, coaxing like, and talked to him, and he turned tail and home he went afore he'd done any harm, and the rest just followed him. How did 'e manage that then? I axed him and he said, 'I tells 'im he was a silly ole duffer to come wandering into a mucky wood, leaving his nice medder, and how every step he took lost him a bite of his own good grass, and he saw sense.' He do have a wonderful way with animals, that's for sure."

That was another thing; at first Miss Blackett had been pleased that Lord Jim and Tom had taken to one another. It was a credit mark for the boy. But, as time went on, she began to resent the cat's marked preference for his company, even above her own. She would not admit that she was so foolish as to be jealous, but what she was beginning to feel was undoubtedly very like jealousy.

When she learned about Tom's picking Mrs Perry's flowers (it was difficult not to hear about things at The Haven), Miss Blackett felt she must apologize to her but Mrs Perry secretly thought that far more harm was done to her treasures by Lord Jim than by Tom.

"I don't really mind, Miss Blackett," she said. "I think he believes all the flowers in the garden belong to us all, himself included, as if we were all one family, I mean, and perhaps too it's because he's used to picking wild flowers wherever and whenever he likes. Anyway, I don't mind at all, so please don't say anything to the boy."

Miss Blackett sniffed. "Much good it would do if I did, with Tom," she thought.

The little incident of the nosegay of pinks, however, made Mrs Perry observe Dorothy Brown more closely.

"Don't you think Miss Brown's changed lately?" she said to

Miss Dawson. "In spite of her deafness, which seems to be getting worse, she's brighter somehow. I don't mean more cheerful exactly, but less of a shadow. One used scarcely to be aware of her. Now, if only it wasn't for that dreadful Miss Ford with her all the time, I believe she could be quite a nice friendly person."

"I can't think why you want everyone to be friendly," said Frances Dawson, though without rancour, adding "but I suppose you can't help it."

"Can it be just Tom's nosegays that have changed her?" mused Mrs Perry, taking no notice of Miss Dawson's remark.

But though Tom's offerings were not without their effect, the change in Dorothy Brown which Mrs Perry had noticed had come about through a completely chance event. Yet this too was connected with the boy. Leila Ford had managed to keep him out of her room by bribing Gisela to do extra cleaning with some of the chocolates she always kept near her, but she could not avoid him altogether. One day, when she and Dorothy were returning to their rooms after dinner, they saw him coming towards them down a passage. Pleased at the meeting and feeling that he had not yet managed to show that he wanted to be friends with Lady Miss Ford, Tom ran towards her with his hand held out in his usual greeting. To her horror Dorothy then saw Leila raise the stick which she now always used to support her great bulk and strike at his outstretched arm, so that it fell to his side.

"Get away – you!" she cried, but Tom stood still. Dorothy, as if impelled by an almost reflex action, immediately stepped up to him and kissed him. Then she went into her own room and shut the door.

At first she was overcome with rage at Leila and surprise at herself. Gradually both anger and surprise faded away. She sat down on her bed ignoring, indeed not even hearing, the imperious tapping on her wall, Leila's customary summons. She knew that something very important had happened to her and that she had to find out what it was. She sat on, and eventually certain facts presented themselves to her. First, that she hated Leila and had done so for years: secondly, that the Leila she had once loved had never existed; thirdly, that Leila had never cared for her and perhaps had never cared for anyone; and lastly, that she had been too cowardly at the beginning and latterly too tired to admit all this to herself. It was as if Leila's stick had struck down not just Tom's arm but the whole false defensive wall that Dorthy had built all these years out of her longing and her pride – a defence against reality. She sat on and felt an extraordinary lightening of spirit. "The truth shall make you free." She knew now something of what these words meant.

Suddenly she became conscious of Leila's insistent renewed angry tapping. She felt emptied of both love and hate and, instead, an immense pity filled her heart. She got up and went to attend to her friend.

Miss Dawson was not much aware of Tom at first. She did not usually care for boys, classing them with cats as the natural enemies of birds. Mary Perry had told her that Tom was a nice boy, but Mary was too apt to think everyone nice. Still, she admitted that as yet she had nothing against him. There had been a native boy on one of her Himalayan trips of whom she had once been quite fond and though he was all grace and this boy was uncouth, yet Tom reminded her of him somehow. They both had the same open, gentle look.

One day, sitting by her window, she heard a sound she hated. It was Lord Jim, yowling triumphantly to let the world know that he had successfully tracked down and caught his prey. The peculiar unmistakable tone of the cry was occasioned by his mouth being full of his wretched victim. Miss Dawson peered out. Yes, there the beast was, carrying what looked very much like another thrush, pitifully quiet and still. Thrushes were especially vulnerable, being slow and trusting birds, and this was the third that she had known Lord Jim take already this summer, and there might of course have been others. Then she saw Tom and so did Lord Jim. He swerved away from the shrubbery where he had intended to deal with his catch privately and at leisure, and instead laid the bird at the feet of Tom, who stooped and picked it up. Miss Dawson called out to him to bring it up to her — she knew that a cat will sometimes carry a bird unharmed until some cover is reached — but she was too far away to make him hear. She saw him holding the thrush quietly in his hands for a little while without moving, then he walked out of sight still holding it, accompanied by Lord Jim, prancing gaily along at his side and waving his tail. As soon as she could, Miss Dawson sent for Tom.

"What did you do with the poor thrush that that wretched cat caught this afternoon?" she asked.

"He be safe and sound, Lady Miss Dawson," said Tom. "He baint hurt at all, only dazed like. I knew where he belongs, down in the copse, there be four on 'em, all from one nest."

"That's a good boy," said Miss Dawson approvingly, "but what about the cat?"

"I'll keep an eye on him," said Tom, "he thought as how I'd be pleased, but he knows now I don't like it. He can't rightly reason it out but he knows. I tell him he gets plenty o' good food given him and there be no need for him to go after the birds at all, but my Gran says once he didn't."

"That's nonsense," said Miss Dawson, "whenever did your grandmother suppose that Miss Blackett didn't overfeed her cat?"

"Not Lady Miss Blackett," said Tom, "but ever so long ago, afore any of us were born, he didn't get fed, so he still thinks he's in the right to catch all he can — but I'll see as he don't get them

72

thrushes."

Miss Dawson was not optimistic all the same, but she felt assured that Tom would try his best to protect the birds and admitted to Mrs Perry that he was a thoroughly well-meaning boy, "Though what he meant about the cat I don't know."

Old Mrs Langley was giving a party. The only visible guest was Tom, but the unseen ones — unseen, that is to say, by all but herself — were the friends and relations she had invited nearly seventy years ago on the occasion of her son's first birthday. Through Tom, who every week took the warden's shopping list to her grocer's and brought back the goods, she had managed to acquire a large chocolate cake and a bottle of sherry. Mrs Langley had happened to meet him when the idea, or memory, or vision of the party had floated into her butterfly mind, and she had firmly added the cake and the sherry to Miss Blackett's list. She had instructed Tom to bring them straight to her. It was Tom, too, who had provided the flowers that filled every vase, and there were a good many of these in Mrs Langley's room. The wild honeysuckle he had found in the copse, but the red roses had come from Fred Mills's beds and the white lilies had been Mrs Perry's pride. The room smelt very sweet.

Mrs Thornton wondered anxiously about all this when she inadvertently also became a guest. She had been passing Mrs Langley's door that afternoon when she heard Tom's unmistakable laugh, and then the quavering sound of Mrs Langley's voice raised louder than usual in one of her favourite hymn tunes. Stopping to listen, Mrs Thornton was able to distinguish the words of "All things bright and beautiful" and then Tom joined in with his humming accompaniment.

"All creatures great and small," trilled out Mrs Langley.

It was really not a wholly inappropriate birthday song, but Mrs Thornton was ignorant of the celebration when first she opened the door and went in. Mrs Langley, looking flushed and joyful, had an empty glass in one hand and was beating time with the other. Tom, too, was waving an empty glass about and on all the little tables scattered round were more empty glasses and plates and the remains of the cake. The room was full of sunlight and flowers and happiness.

"Come in, come in, dear Jessie, but mind baby; he crawls around so fast now, he is always getting under people's feet. Come in and drink his health."

Mrs Thornton, however, could not drink his health for there was obviously no more sherry left. She sat down and, as usual, Mrs Langley's fantasies of the past began to affect her powerfully. Just as once she had thought that she heard the trotting of horses bringing Mrs Langley's young husband to the door of The Haven, so now she could almost visualize the guests to whom Tom was handing round the diminished cake, as grave and as absorbed as if he were a child in one of those universal games of playing at grown-ups. She could even imagine the lively one-year-old, the centre of the party, that baby who was now a frail old gentleman with a stomach ulcer living unhappily in Birmingham with his successful stockbroker son.

"Now, my precious," said Mrs Langley, bending down, "it's time for bath and bed, birthday or no birthday, and you, Dickie —" she called Tom Dickie because that had been the name of Susan's boy — "take these glasses down to the pantry and wash them very carefully, for they were a wedding present and a lovely present, too."

She went off to the bathroom and Tom disappeared with the glasses. Mrs Thornton knew these well, beautiful cut-glass ones, which lived on the top shelf of the corner cupboard above the Worcester teacups. Unfortunately, when Tom was bringing back the glasses after he had washed them, he met the warden.

"What are you doing with those?" she asked him.

"They're from Lady Mrs Langley's party," said Tom.

"Party, what party?"

74

"Lady Mrs Langley's been having a party," repeated Tom.

"Nonsense," said Miss Blackett, and followed him into Mrs Langley's room. Mrs Thornton had gone and Mrs Langley, having returned from the bathroom, had gone immediately and peacefully to sleep.

"I can smell alcohol," said Miss Blackett loudly and sharply. "You know alcohol, unless specially prescribed, is against the rules, Mrs Langley; how did you get it?"

Mrs Langley, so suddenly wakened, looked frightened and bewildered.

"Dickie got it for my party," she said.

"There was *no* party," said Miss Blackett, "and, Tom, you must never get anything for the ladies without asking me about it first, do you understand?"

Tom first nodded his head and then shook it.

Miss Blackett sighed and went straight away to write to Mrs Langley's grandson, which she had been meaning to do ever since the committee meeting. She wrote:

Dear Mr Langley,

I fear your grandmother's state has deteriorated so that we cannot any longer give her all the care she needs. We are anxious that she should be better looked after in the very efficient geriatric unit of the local hospital than she can be at The Haven. If you could make it convenient to come here as soon as possible you will be able to judge the situation for yourself and if, as I am sure will be the case, you concur with our proposal to move your grandmother, I hope you will arrange for the disposal of her property. I believe your father's state of health makes it impossible for him to act in this matter.

Yours sincerely,
Agnes Blackett.

Mr Langley, being one of those to whom time is money, did not find it convenient to visit his grandmother nor, for that matter, had he ever done so. But he saw the necessity now, so he came down to The Haven not too long after receiving this letter.

Mrs Langley greeted him politely but without enthusiasm as her Uncle James. "I am glad to see you looking so well, Uncle," she said, "though I don't know to what I owe the pleasure of this unexpected visit. Now that I am a married woman I can confess that I once overheard you telling my father that I was disgracefully indulged and you made no secret of the fact that you dislike my dear husband. Still," she added hopefully, "perhaps you have had a change of heart."

"I must agree with you, Miss Blackett," said Mr Langley after this uncomfortable interview, "my poor grandmother is quite senile. It will be much better for all concerned if she can be placed in a suitable institution. I will arrange for her things to be sold, there are some quite good pieces among them I noticed, but my wife does not care for antiques. I must thank you on behalf of my father and myself for all the care you have taken of her since she came to The Haven — and now, if you will forgive me, I must be off. Good day to you, Miss Blackett, you will hear from me again shortly."

During the weeks since Tom's arrival at The Haven, Miss Norton had been feeling increasingly depressed; her eyes had been failing more rapidly than had been predicted, and the doctor had told her there was nothing to be done. Up to now she had not faced the possibility of total loss of sight. She could still distinguish light and darkness and dimly see large shapes of people and furniture, and if she looked obliquely and closely at an object, it became sufficiently clear for her to discern its nature. For instance, peering sideways across the dining-room table, she could tell a sugar basin from a jug, though it was a hazardous job to pour the contents of the jug into a cup or sprinkle the sugar on a plate. She could not bring herself to accept dependence on others for personal intimate services. She felt that death would be more welcome than utter blindness and helplessness and, when the time came, she told herself, there were ways of putting an end to things. A plastic bag would be the easiest; she believed she had the courage for this, though not for long years of darkness and decline. She began to set herself tests over and above the ordinary daily tasks. If she passed these tests she went to bed reasonably content.

One morning, however, she woke with a headache and a feeling of oppression and fancied herself distinctly less able to deal with washing, dressing and breakfast. Spurred on by a sudden onslaught of fear, she decided to set herself a more severe and hazardous test that day. She would walk to the end of the garden and through the copse alone, something she had not done for weeks. She chose her time carefully. It must be after the midday meal when nearly everyone rested and there was little fear of interfering warnings or help. After she had made this decision she felt quite calm and she set off at the right time and aided by her stick, with which she struck at the little iron edging to the gravel path, she successfully negotiated the long lawn and came to the boundary between this and the wood. Originally this had been a ditch which by now was almost filled up, but the path into the copse still crossed it by an old rustic bridge. The invading bullocks had lately broken down the wooden handrail of the bridge and, as the ditch was now almost level and the rail was scarcely needed any more, and as Fred always had more jobs than he could cope with, it had not been replaced. Meg Norton reached the bridge and followed the path across, but midway her stick failed to find any guiding rail and she halted. She could just make out the shapes of the trees looming up before her, then they seemed to advance and engulf her and panic seized her. She could no longer pierce the darkness and she felt it would be a step into a void and that this void was endless. She had been too engrossed in carrying out her plan to heed the weather, but it had turned colder at midday, clouds had gathered and it now began to rain. A plane roared overhead and to Meg it sounded like thunder and added to her distress. She had always hated thunder. She felt as terrified as if she were a child again, caught up in a nightmare and trying to call aloud for her mother, only no call would come. She forced herself to take a step, caught her foot on a little stump and fell. Then she must have cried out, she supposed, for there came a voice shouting her name and out of the blackness a pair of small, strong hands took hold of her and pulled her to her feet. Tom had been in the wood spying on his family of thrushes and had heard her. She clung to him.

"Why, Lady Miss Norton dear, be you hurt?" he asked.

The warmth of his arm about her and the sound of his voice brought immediate comfort and relief. She was so glad it was Tom who had found her, she somehow did not mind *him* seeing her so helpless and frightened.

"It was silly," she said, "I came for a walk and fell. I'm going blind, Tom, you see. I *am* blind," she added loudly and firmly.

"Like my bats," said Tom cheerfully. He began to tell her about the bats as he led her back to the house. It was still raining.

"'Tis a good bit o' rain," said Tom. "Don't our flowers smell happy?"

Meg became aware of the summer scents jostling each other for her attention and a fresh warm tide of life seemed to flow through her. When she got to her room she asked Tom if he could bring her a cup of tea, and she lay down on the bed for, though not hurt, she was shaken by the fall and her fear. But when evening was come, she was quite able to go into supper and then she asked Mrs Perry, her neighbour, for the first time,

78

to help her with her food and to pour out her drink, and Mrs Perry, who had been longing to do this for weeks past but had not dared to offer, did so without comment. It was one of Mrs Thornton's days for reading to Meg, and she went to her room as soon as supper was over. Shakespeare took his turn as usual after *The Times*. They were in the middle of *As You Like It* but this evening Meg said: "Would you mind if instead we had that bit near the end of *King Lear* about Edgar as poor mad Tom, with Gloucester." So Mrs Thornton found the place and came at length to Gloucester's speech.

> "Alack, I have no eyes,
>   Is wretchedness deprived that benefit
>   To end itself by death?
> *Edgar:* Give me your arm.
>   Up! so, How is't feel your legs? You stand alone?
> *Glouc.:* I do remember, now henceforth I'll bear
>   Affliction, till it do cry out itself
>   Enough, enough and die.
> *Edgar:* Bear free and patient thoughts."

Mrs Thornton read on and Meg lay back in her chair and listened.

> *Glouc.:* "You ever gentle gods, take my breath from me,
>   Let not my worser spirit tempt me again
>   To die before you please."

And so at last she came to Edgar's final words to his father:

> "Men must endure
>   Their going hence, even as their coming hither,
>   Ripeness is all."

Here Mrs Thornton paused as she thought she heard Meg speak. "Did you say something?" she asked.

"Only what comes next, I think," said Meg: " 'And that's true too.' "

"Shall I finish the play?" asked Mrs Thornton.

"No, thank you, dear," said Meg, "I'm rather tired this evening, so I think I'll go up to bed now, but thank you very much and goodnight."

7

PREPARATIONS FOR THE FETE

MISS BLACKETT was anxious to move Mrs Langley to the geriatric department at the hospital before the day of the summer fête and was pleased when she heard, soon after Mr Langley's visit, that a bed was vacant. The matron rang her up to tell her this and Miss Blackett expressed relief.

"I shall be very busy soon," she said, "for our great day is coming along and I really cannot supervise the old thing, day in and day out, and yet I feel responsible, of course."

"I quite understand," said Matron crisply, "right, well, I daresay I can save you the trouble of bringing her along. We don't use an ambulance unless it's necessary, but I have to come your way in my own car the day after tomorrow and could pick her up about noon, if you can have her ready by then."

Miss Blackett agreed to this.

"I suppose she'll come without trouble?"

"Oh, yes," said Miss Blackett, "she's quite an amenable old soul."

"Right," said Matron, "it's as well to know — we have our obstinate little ways sometimes. About noon, then, Miss Blackett. Goodbye."

It was not quite as easy as Miss Blackett had hoped.

"Come along now, my dearie," said Matron, "we're going to take you for a nice drive."

"But I don't know you," said Mrs Langley, drawing back. "My name is Mrs Marian Langley," she added with dignity.

"That's right, dear," said Matron, "and we're going for a lovely drive together."

Miss Blackett was busy fastening down a suitcase which was difficult to shut and just then Tom came in with a message for her. Mrs Langley caught at his hand.

"Can Dickie come too?" she asked.

The matron looked over his head at Miss Blackett and gave a little nod. "Very well," said Miss Blackett.

"Right," said Matron, "let's be moving then, shall we?"

But when they got downstairs and out into the drive, she propelled Mrs Langley into the car and shut the door, leaving Tom on the steps. Mrs Langley's attention was distracted by the bright red cushions on her seat and by a mascot of a toy panda tied to the windscreen, and she forgot about Tom until the engine started. Then she leaned out of the window and called to him.

"Never mind, Dickie, you must come next time, tell your mother, please, to have tea ready, I'll be back very soon." She waved and Tom waved too till she was out of sight.

But she was not back soon. Instead, Mr Langley's secretary came down with a man from a Birmingham firm of auctioneers and took away all the furniture, pictures, china and glass, packing the last very carefully and with respect.

"Where be Lady Mrs Langley gone?" Tom asked Mrs Thornton. "And when be she coming home again?"

"She won't be coming home," said Mrs Thornton, "she's had to go into hospital, Tom."

"She weren't in bed," said Tom, "she were going for a ride."

"I know, Tom," said Mrs Thornton, "but she had to go to hospital all the same, the doctor said so, and you see all her things are gone — she wouldn't want to come back to an empty room, would she?"

Tom looked puzzled but shook his head in agreement. He went away humming Mrs Langley's favourite hymn tune, which didn't now seem so appropriate as at the party. He was heard humming it several times in the days that followed, though he did not speak of her again. But Mrs Thornton noticed a curious thing: whenever he passed Mrs Langley's door in future, he always went on tiptoe.

Mrs Thornton asked the vicar on his next visit if he had been to see Mrs Langley yet, and how she was.

"Matron says she's fine, she's put on weight and she gives no trouble at all, but I found her very quiet, very quiet indeed. I'm sorry," he added, "but the committee and the warden all thought it was the right and sensible thing to do."

Mrs Thornton said nothing.

With Mrs Langley off her hands, Miss Blackett was free to concentrate on arrangements for the fête. She had decided that the deodar tree could not come down until this was over. It would make too much of a mess. A sub-committee consisting of herself, Mrs Mitchell, the vicar's wife, and Col. Bradshaw was due to meet to discuss all arrangements. The weather seemed settled at last.

"It's bound to be fine now we've decided on the marquee instead of a band," Miss Blackett said to Mrs Perry and Miss Dawson, who were sitting on one of the garden seats watching Tom watering the rosebeds. Watering was one of the few gardening jobs Fred could give him to do when he could be spared by Miss Blackett. Weeding was out of the question for he obstinately refused to pull up anything.

"They be all as good as one another to him – dandelions and daisies, just as vallible as roses and lilies," grumbled Fred. But he loved watering. When he had finished the rosebeds he came over to give Mrs Perry's border its turn. He was humming loudly and happily a Schubert song he had heard on Mrs Thornton's radio the evening before.

"That boy's a band in himself," said Miss Dawson. It was then Mrs Perry had her bright idea.

"I don't see why we shouldn't have a band of sorts at the fête," she said. "My grandson and his sister play in a music group, I know they went all over the place playing last summer. I believe they would come and play for us here if they were asked. Tom could help, too, I'm sure. It would be lovely to have them, and much more fun than a hired band."

Miss Blackett looked doubtful.

"We wouldn't want pop music, you know, Mrs Perry, and would they really want to give up the time, we couldn't pay them."

"Oh, I'm sure they'd come if they were free," said Mrs Perry confidently. "Austen is always ready for anything, and Nell's boyfriend Jake is very musical, properly musical, I mean, so it wouldn't have to be pop. I'm certain they wouldn't mind giving up the time. Why, you know Nell and Austen, Miss Blackett, you know they wouldn't."

No one at The Haven could help knowing about Mrs Perry's grandchildren, not to speak of her great-grandchildren. What space in her room that could be spared from her plants was taken up with photographs of them at many different stages. She had five altogether, and now three greats, but Nell and Austen were familiar in person to everyone as they quite frequently came to see her. Austen was in his second year at Oxford and Nell, who had taken an art course and painted flowers really well, had a job in an art gallery in Warwick. She shared a flat with Jake, who was doing a postgraduate course at Warwick University. They talked vaguely of marriage at some distant date.

"I don't approve, of course," said Mrs Perry cheerfully, "but it doesn't really matter."

"If you don't approve, I don't see how you can say it doesn't matter," said Miss Dawson.

Mrs Perry ignored this; she often found it better to take no notice of Frances's remarks when they seemed irrelevant.

Miss Blackett liked Austen Perry, who always made a point of seeing her when he came. Nell she thought aloof and superior. After some consideration she agreed to put Mrs Perry's suggestion before the sub-committee and they reacted favourably.

Mrs Mitchell said it was really very sweet of Mrs Perry to think of it.

Col. Bradshaw said: "I've met those grandchildren of hers, an attractive pair. If they will come, I think we can trust them to provide a suitable programme, though perhaps we'd better vet it. It's good to involve young people in charitable affairs whenever possible."

Miss Blackett said: "Well, it would certainly be nice to have some music after all, but I shan't be surprised if it doesn't come off. You can't rely on the young nowadays, so I don't think we should count on it."

Mrs Perry, however, certainly did count on it, and so it was that when Austen Perry looked through his mail one morning, he picked out from the customary bills and circulars an envelope adressed in his grandmother's distinctive pointed script. He enjoyed her letters, she wrote just as if she were chatting away to him about her plants, and the family news, and amiable gossip concerning The Haven. This was a fatter letter than usual. It gave an account of Tom's rout of the bullocks, which amused him, and then came to the fête and the real purpose of the epistle.

I know you and Nell will help if you can. There won't be any money in it for you, I'm afraid, because, as I've explained, we can't afford a band this year; you had better make this clear to your friends, but I'm sure as they are your friends and bound to be nice, they won't mind, but they'll get a good tea with strawberries and cream, and they might win a raffle prize – I think we ought to let you have tickets free. If you can come, would you mind sending a list of what you are going to play. I know it will all be delightful, but they seem to want to know beforehand, at least Col. Bradshaw and Miss Blackett do, or better than sending it, perhaps you could run over here one day soon. It seems a long while since I saw you, but you've been hard at work, I expect.

And she remained his "very loving Gran".

Austen smiled and pondered a little and then went to his phone and dialled Nell.

"I've had a letter."

"From Gran?" interrupted his sister. "So have I, about playing at their fête."

"Just so, what do you think?"

"I'll have to ask Jake and he's asleep at the moment, but I don't really see why not. I've got nothing on that weekend, what about you?"

"I can make it, who else can we get hold of?"

"We simply must have Elizabeth, is she up still?"

The vac. had begun, but there were always undergraduates still around for one purpose or another, among whom was Austen himself, who liked to get a little work done after the hurly burly of the term was ended.

"In between her conferences and protest marches and meetings, she is," he answered Nell.

"Well, even if we can't get hold of anyone else, the four of us ought to manage something, but we must get together pretty soon if we're to do it. What about bringing Elizabeth here for a night? You've been promising to come for ages."

"Good thought. I'll make a point of seeing Liz at once and ring you. Love to Jake – goodbye for now." Austen replaced the receiver, finished his breakfast and decided to stroll across the Parks to Elizabeth's lodgings then and there. Early morning was the safest time to find people at home, even if still in bed.

However, Elizabeth came to the door at once in a particularly fine dressing-gown, though her hair was hanging in wet strands over her face. She was a handsome, dark-complexioned girl, with large prominent brown eyes and a determined mouth and chin. Her bed-sitting-room was untidy by any standards; everything, clothes, cooking utensils, food, were all mixed up with piles of books, and cascades of paper appeared to be spilling themselves over the whole collection. The only object that seemed to have a proper place was a fiddle on a shelf to itself. Elizabeth was an able violinist. Austen cleared a space on the floor and sat down. Elizabeth remained standing and, seizing up a towel from a heap of mixed garments, started to rub her hair with extreme vigour. Austen gave her the gist of his grandmother's letter and his talk with Nell.

"No, I'm afraid I'm booked for an anti-nuclear demonstration that day. Sorry."

"Oh, come off it, Liz, it can't really affect the peace of the world all that much if you are there or not, and you're indispensable to us."

"He who would do good, must do it in minute particulars," quoted Elizabeth.

"Don't be sententious, besides, come to that, I bet Blake would be on our side; think of all the certain good you can do in the minute particulars waiting for us to perform at The Haven – whereas!" he shrugged his shoulders.

"But I promised," said Liz.

"Well, will you come if I find you a sub.?" asked Austen.

Elizabeth felt herself weakening. She was dismayed to find how unpleasant it was to hold out again him – it would be inconveniently hampering to fall for him in a serious way, and she feared she might be going to. "I suppose so," she said unwillingly, "but you ought to be demonstrating yourself."

"We'll argue that out on our way to Nell and Jake," said Austen cheerfully. "Thanks a lot, Liz, I'm sure I can find someone. Be seeing you – goodbye, then."

Austen possessed a wide and devoted circle of friends and it was not too difficult to persuade one of them to take Elizabeth's place at the demonstration. "It's lucky it's for a respectable cause," he thought, "and not one of her way-out crazes."

So, her conscience more or less appeased, Elizabeth packed herself and her violin into Austen's shabby little car the following weekend, and immediately embarked on an argument on unilateral disarmament. They were still arguing when they drew up outside Nell and Jake's flat in Warwick. Nell received them joyfully. The flat possessed a fair-sized living-room, a tiny kitchen and bathroom, a double bedroom and one small spare room containing a large mattress that was scarcely ever vacant.

"Oh, by the way," said Nell to her brother at supper, "I hope you won't mind sharing your bed with a nice Irish roadsweeper – we're putting him up till he can find a lodging."

"That's all right," said Austen. "He won't be drunk, I hope?"

There were limits beyond which he was not prepared to go. "Where's Liz to sleep then?"

"She'll have Jake's side of my bed and he'll be quite OK on the living-room floor, won't you, Jake?"

"Of course," said Jake.

The flat was a pleasant place, tidy and clean and decorated with some of Nell's flower paintings. Her appearance was deceptive, she was very slim and small, with delicate features and a cloud of silvery fair hair. She looked like a cross between a Botticelli angel and a character from a de la Mare poem. But, in

88

reality, both she and Austen were more efficient and practical than either Elizabeth, the idealist, or Jake, the mathematical mystic. Neither Nell or Jake were great talkers, but the other pair made up for this. At supper they started a vigorous debate on the ethics of space travel. Nell listened a little anxiously. Austen, she knew, argued for entertainment and was quite capable of changing sides at any moment, but Liz was always in deadly earnest and Nell felt, rather than consciously thought, that at least where Austen was concerned, she was emotionally involved. She was glad that she and Jake seldom felt the need to argue, but went their own ways in peace and comfort. She went out to fetch a jug of coffee and when she came back the argument had somehow shifted to Wagner.

"You're prejudiced against him, just because of his politics," Austen was saying. "Genius has nothing to do with politics."

"It jolly well had with Wagner," said Elizabeth, "and you're not fair either; it isn't just his politics, I hate the way he forces me to respond to his beastly genius, for I can't help responding. It makes me feel I'm being raped."

"I understand what Liz means," said Jake, "Wagner always wants total control, that's the great difference between him and Bach, his opposite. Bach is content to accept divine control."

Elizabeth looked at him with gratitude, and Nell said, "We've got a new cassette of Tortelier playing Bach's cello suite. Let's get down to business and then we'll play it to you. Now what shall we choose out of our repertoire for the fête?"

"The old will want something nostalgic, I should think," said Elizabeth.

"Don't talk about 'the old' like that," said Austen, "as though they were all alike and some sort of different species. They're as different from one another as can be, as we are, for instance – we're not just 'the young'. Generalizations are always stupid."

"You've just made one," said Elizabeth, "and a stupid one,

too. Of course I know they can be wrong, even dangerous sometimes, but one can't do without them all the same."

"Why not?" said Austen.

"Oh, stop it, you two," said Nell, "and let's get on. It isn't only old ladies we've got to please, Liz, this fête tries to attract everyone it can."

She was sorting through a pile of music she had taken from a drawer and arranging it in neat piles. Their group had gone busking last summer vacation and besides had performed at weekends in pubs and sometimes at parties during the winter, and Jake had orchestrated a fair amount of material for them. The piles represented Old Time, pop and classical. After a good deal of discussion, they decided on Highlights from Gilbert & Sullivan, and Selections from Strauss Waltzes. "That's for Gran," said Austen. Then Gershwin's "Summertime", the Beatles' "Eight Days a Week", and "Yesterday".

"We're not allowed pop, I know," said Nell, "but the Beatles don't count as pop, do they?"

"That's for 'the young', I suppose," said Liz.

"Selections from *Fledermaus* — that ought to be for everyone," said Nell.

"We must have something from the classical heap," said Jake. "What about Mozart's 'Eine Kleine Nachtmuzik', or Handel's 'Water Music'?"

"We do the Mozart best," said Austen, "and we ought to have a rousing number to start off with."

They decided on the "Toreador's Song" from *Carmen*.

"That ought to do all right," said Nell, "but I wish we had a singer. Sarah's gone off to her beloved Austria; what's happened to Andrew?"

"He's taken a job as a dustman," said Austen. "He says it's horribly exhausting, but very good money. I vote for some Bach now, it's too late to start practising tonight. We'll get down to it

90

tomorrow morning."

They relaxed comfortably while Tortelier did his best for them and then, full of content, they sought their beds.

Austen found Mike, the sweeper, already snoring but considerately squeezed into as narrow a space as possible on the far side of the mattress. He slipped in beside him and Mike was up and away before he woke the next day. The morning was spent in hard but pleasurable playing. Besides Elizabeth's fiddle, there was Jake's double bass, Nell provided the wind with her clarinet, and Austen performed quite creditably on the guitar, but there was no doubt that a vocal accompaniment to some of the numbers would have been an improvement.

"Can't be helped, unless we can pick up someone between now and the day — we must just do the best we can without," said Nell.

Mrs Perry proudly told everyone that her grandchildren had undertaken to provide music for the fête instead of the Boys' Brigade Band, and that Austen was paying her a visit soon to discuss it all. Austen was popular at The Haven. He possessed the art, or rather the gift (for it came naturally) of talking to children, his parents' contemporaries, and the old, as if they were all the same age as himself. Then, because he was interested in people, he remembered the old ladies' names, and often, too, bits of information about them that Mrs Perry had told him. He arrived at The Haven one Sunday with a miniature rose-tree in a pot for his grandmother, and a box of chocolates with a picture of a ginger cat on it, for Miss Blackett. She was more pleased with this than even Mrs Perry with her plant, though no one would have guessed it, for she had never learned to accept gifts graciously. She liked chocolates, but never bought them for herself, and she liked the picture of the cat, even though it was not handsome enough for Lord Jim, but best of all she liked the attention and the box was kept long after its contents had been consumed.

Austen had arrived in time for the midday meal and afterwards he tried to persuade his grandmother to take her usual nap.

"I can go for a walk, or talk to Miss Blackett."

"What, snooze away an hour of your company, I should think not indeed! We'll sit outside in the garden and you can admire my border while you tell me all your news. Oh, and I want to hear what nice tunes you have all decided on, though I don't suppose I'll know any of them."

"You will two of them, anyway, for we've put them in specially for you, Gran. Here's the list."

Mrs Perry put on her spectacles.

"Hurrah! Gilbert and Sullivan, and the Vienna Waltzes – good boy, and I like the names of the songs, 'Summertime' and 'Yesterday', they sound like those that were sung when I was young."

"I'm afraid they're not much like that really, and they won't be sung, you know, only played, because we've lost both our singers, and haven't been able to find any replacement. I say, Gran, your pinks and stocks are fine this year, but what's happened to your famous tiger lilies?"

"Tom's happened to them," said Mrs Perry ruefully, "he borrowed every single one of them for a party dear old Mrs Langley thought she was giving and it has left rather a gap."

"Tom, Tom, the piper's son, stole your flowers and away did run," sang Austen. "Only he's not a piper's son, but a bullock boy, according to your letter. Tell me more about him – he sounds quite a one."

"He's really a very nice boy," said Mrs Perry, "and clever at a lot of things, though he's never been able to read or write. Mrs Thornton says he's exceptionally musical."

"Oh, ho!" said Austen, "does he sing, I wonder?"

92

"Not sing, exactly," said Mrs Perry, "but he hums quite loudly and Mrs Thornton says he always keeps in time and in tune. Oh, do you think he might be of any use to you, Austen? I wondered if possibly he might, he would love it so."

"I'd better see Mrs Thornton about him," said Austen, "a champion hummer might be a novel draw."

"I do approve of you, Austen dear," said his grandmother affectionately, "you're always ready to try anything, and I love you so much better now you have your hair nice and short and tidy again. I couldn't bear it hanging down your back like a Cavalier, which is funny really, as I always liked Cavaliers better than Roundheads, but then you didn't wear a lace collar and a beautiful coat underneath, and perhaps that made the difference."

"Oh, Gran, you never said you hated it," said Austen.

"Well, that wouldn't have been any use, would it, dear?"

"The parents thought it would, they were always on about it."

"Yes, and I believe you grew it an inch longer whenever the poor dears mentioned it. I told them they only had to wait a little and the fashion would pass, they always do, though sometimes they come back again."

Mrs Thornton guaranteed that Tom could pick up tunes wonderfully well, but that he might wander away in the middle if he felt like it.

"Of course we'd have to get him to practise with us first," said Austen, "is he shy?"

"Oh no, not in the least," said Mrs Thornton.

"We could get here early in the day and the fête's an afternoon affair, isn't it? We could practise him in the morning."

"But the warden will need him then, I'm afraid," said Mrs Thornton, "there will be plenty of jobs for him to do."

"I'll ask her anyway," said Austen, "where is he now? I'd like to see him."

"He always goes home on a Sunday and doesn't come back till Monday morning."

"Oh, well, I'll take your word for his musical powers, Mrs Thornton, and I bet I get Miss Blackett's permission to rehearse him, you'll see."

He sought out the warden then and there, and perhaps it was the effect of the chocolate box, but, to Mrs Thornton's surprise, permission was given by Miss Blackett for Tom to give up at least part of the morning to practise with the group if they really wanted him, though she couldn't believe that he would be of any real use, but then she didn't pretend to understand anything about music and never had.

"That's marvellous of you, Miss Blackett," said Austen. "If he's as good as Mrs Thornton says he is, he'll be just what we need in some of the numbers, and I promise you we'll help all we can when we're not actually playing to make up for robbing you of Tom."

When they next met together the group approved of including Tom, but cautious Nell said it would be advisable if Jake, who had the most time to spare at present, could run over to The Haven on his bike as soon as possible to try him out.

Jake came back a bit worried. "Isn't he any good after all?" asked Nell.

"He's fine," said Jake.

"What's the problem, then?"

"Too keen," said Jake, "we can't have him humming every number, not the Mozart, for instance, and he will if he gets the chance."

"I see," said Nell, thoughtfully. "Well, can't we give him an instrument, cymbals or something, to keep him happy and un-humming?"

"It's more than likely he'd be too keen on those, too," said Jake. "Can you imagine trying to compete with clanging cymbals coming in with every beat?"

"What about a drum?" said Nell, "That wouldn't really matter if it went on rather a lot. I can borrow a little drum from Earl Street Primary School."

"Just the thing; he'd love it," said Jake with relief, "and I think we could make it clear to him when to hum and when to drum."

"What shall we wear?" mused Nell. "I think something pretty eye-catching. I saw some cheap red and white denim the other day in the town. I could run up dungarees for Liz and myself to wear with white blouses, and you've got your red shirt, and I think Austen's got one too, at least I know he's got a check one, and you can wear white flannels with them."

"What about Tom?" asked Jake.

"Oh, I can run him up something, too, or we could buy him something. How big is he?"

"About your size, I should think," said Jake, "but best lend him some of your things – don't you know it's dangerous to give new clothes to elemental creatures such as Tom."

Nell laughed. "Is he a changeling then, d'you think, or a sort of Brownie, or Lob?"

"I don't know," said Jake, suddenly becoming half serious, "all I know is that I felt he was different, as if he knew things I didn't know and saw things I couldn't see, and was timeless somehow."

Nell smiled at him affectionately. She loved Jake when he talked nonsense.

Other matters connected with the fête were not going quite so well. There were the coconut shies, for instance. Mr Jackson always took charge of these. The site had to be far enough away from the house and the stalls to avoid damage, but this meant that balls were often mislaid in the rough patch between the lawn and the copse, or even in the copse itself, unless the nets were sound. This year, it was found that, though the stands stored in the old barn were all right, the nets had been used by Fred for some purpose of his own and had several holes in them. This led to a few words between him and the farmer, their relationship never being very warm on account of the bullocks. Then the coconuts, provided by the local greengrocer, had proved unsatisfactory the previous summer – almost a quarter were bad and there had been loud complaints, so this year Jackson had gone elsewhere for his coconuts. This gave offence and the greengrocer, who last year had sold the strawberries for the fête at a discount, quietly increased his price without notification.

There was always some bickering and jealousy between the old ladies' stall and a similar fancy goods stall run by the Women's Institute, who donated a part of their takings to The Haven in return for the privilege of selling their articles at the fête, and the competition for the best sites was not too amiable either sometimes. This summer the sudden spell of hot weather made the shady places in the garden especially sought after.

The sub-committee resigned themselves to the inevitable annoyances and frets and trusted that, as usual, everything would work out pretty well in the end. The stallholders were traditional and seldom changed from year to year. However, this time Col. Bradshaw, still mindful of Miss Hughes's financial assets, suggested that it might be as well to involve her yet further in The Haven's affairs by allotting to her the privilege and pleasure of one of the stalls. The other members of the sub-committee looked doubtful. How could this be done without causing trouble?

Someone suggested an extra stall. "What about a White Elephant Stall? We've never had one before."

Someone else said there would be enough white elephants already on the other stalls and that Miss Hughes was proving a bit of a one herself. It was a long, hot meeting and in order to bring it to an end, objections faded out and it was decided to adopt the idea of a White Elephant Stall to be presided over by Miss Hughes.

As the day approached, all the talk at The Haven was about the fête and, among other matters, the White Elephant Stall was discussed.

"I can't rightly see as there'll be room for them on our lawn," said Tom to Gisela, anxiously. "I've seed elephants once in a picture Teacher showed us at school and they do be bigger nor any other animal, and they be grey and not white."

"It must be that you heard wrong about the Stall, Tom, certainly there will be no room and the elephants, they *are* grey and not white at all, but the English are strange about colour, I find," said Gisela.

But Tom was sure he had heard right, and asked Mrs Thornton, who was his oracle, and she explained, as best she could, the genius and purpose of a White Elephant Stall. The following day she was a little puzzled at a sudden cross-examination from Tom about her furniture.

"Lady Mrs Thornton, be all these things yourn?"

"Why, yes, Tom."

"All the tables and chairs and the pictures and all they books? Be they yourn as you can do whatever you like with 'em?"

"Certainly."

"Be all the ladies' things as are in their rooms theirs?"

"Yes, just the same as mine are."

Mrs Thornton thought of Tom's behaviour with regard to the flowers in the garden and that perhaps he had been getting into trouble with Fred or the warden again. Perhaps a word or two at this moment as regards personal property might be opportune.

"At The Haven, in the garden and in the dining- and sitting-room and the hall and the kitchen, Tom, everything is for us all

97

to use and enjoy, and no one of us must take any of the things that are in these places away for their own use. But in our separate rooms, it is different, everything there belongs to the owner of the room as my things belong to me to do what I like with – do you understand now?"

Tom nodded and then crowed his sudden happy laugh and disappeared.

8

THE FÊTE

EARLY ON the morning of the fête a thick, white mist blotted out the landscape, then, gradually, the sun forced its way through. The black August tree tops appeared first and soon the swathes of vapour cleared off, leaving the lawn and the field beyond the copse sparkling and fresh. Everything was extraordinarily still and silent. Through Meg Norton's open window came the gentle scent of mown grass. Fred had been busy with the mower all the day before. Time was arbitrary at The Haven; often it ceased to be regulated by clocks and watches and took its cue from scents and sounds. So now, Meg, half-awake and half-dozing, smelt the summer of seventy years ago. It was the day of the annual cricket match against Widford. Harry and Paul were both playing and her father captaining the village team. She would help at the scoring board and with the tea. Of course they would win and afterwards there would be a party at the Hall. Oh, it was going to be a lovely, lovely day.

Only why was it so dark on an August morning? Even if she had forgotten to draw back the curtains last night (which she never did, for she liked to see the night sky), but even if she had, it ought not to be so dark as this. She sat up, still only half-awake, and then time swung on again and she remembered. Still, that day had been lived, that perfect day – nothing could alter that now – it was as real as this one and hers for ever. She went on thinking about it and smiling as she thought. It all happened as she had expected. Harry had carried his bat and Paul had made one marvellous catch, and though poor father had been out for a duck, he didn't mind, for they won by 46 runs. She remembered the exact number and at the party she had worn her new Shantung silk dress and her greeny-blue Venetian beads, and Mummy had let her do her pigtail up in a doorknocker for the first time, with a big bow to match the beads – though she wasn't "out" yet, of course. Monica, her cousin, was staying with them. She married a doctor, he joined the RAMC and they went out to India afterwards and Monica died there. Yes, Monica was with them and after supper, they had rolled up the carpet and Mummy had played waltzes – "the Valse Triste", she could hear it now. She had danced a lot with Paul and he had told her she had the most wonderful eyes, which made her feel silly, but she knew Harry was pleased that she and Paul got on well together. It must have been three years before the War. Here her musings were interrupted by Gisela bringing in her breakfast – Gisela, who was German, and whose grandfather and father had both been killed in the Wars.

"It is the day of the fête, Miss Norton," said Gisela, "and it will be a very fine day, I think."

"I'm glad, Gisela," said Meg. "Be happy and enjoy it."

Mrs Perry ate her breakfast by her open window, the moisture from the mist was drying off quickly from the ground now and all the later summer colours were solid and thick, like oil paint. Beyond the dark copse was the bright cornfield. Soon the proud upstanding wheat would be reduced to square lifeless packets.

"You never see a lovely wheatsheaf now," mourned Mrs Perry, "unless it's made of bread and propped against the chancel screen at Harvest Festival."

But Fred admired the packets. He was busy tidying up the

100

mess the men had made erecting the marquee.

"And then those hateful stubble fires," thought Mrs Perry. She leaned out of the window and called to Fred: "Is Mr Jackson going to burn his stubble this summer, Fred? One summer he didn't."

Fred straightened himself up to answer her. "That'd be by reason o' the drought, in case o' fire," he said. "I reckon he'll be burning this year, same as usual."

"Such a waste," sighed Mrs Perry, "when I was a girl we went gleaning."

"Depends how you looks at it, ma'am," said Fred. "It saves work and it saves time."

"And then the flowers," went on Mrs Perry, "the flowers that sprang up immediately after the harvesting, cornflowers, and poppies, and mayweed, and scarlet pimpernel, and yellow bedstraw and speedwell – a perfect carpet."

"Nobbut weeds," muttered Fred. "Well, I'd best be getting on – them marquee men've mucked up my edges a caution."

At ten o'clock Fred's brother's wife arrived to help in the kitchen. Fred's wife called her "Old Misery". She was cockney born and bred. As she unpacked the china, lent for the teas, she held Gisela with her "glittering eye" like the Ancient Mariner, while she regaled her with intimate details about her family (though actually her eye was glassy rather than glittering).

"My grandfather 'ad eighteen children, 'e 'ad, and only reared four. My father, 'e was 'is only son and 'es niver bin right since 'e married, the doctors 'ave niver bin able to do nothing for 'im. My mother, she was five weeks late wiv me and the old cat died the very day I was born, the very same day, she did, and they say she was a lovely cat, too. My mother she went sudden like. It was my washing day, if I'd 'a known she was going I'd 'ave got the washing done before."

Then the warden came in. "You shouldn't be standing here

101

talking when there's so much to do," she said crossly to Gisela. "Go and help Tom put up the tables in the marquee."

Gisela went off aggrieved – it wasn't her that was doing the talking, but Miss Blackett was not in a state to be fair.

Now the stallholders were beginning to arrive to stake out their territory, erect their stalls and assemble their goods. Honor Bredon, who was in charge of the old ladies' stall, went round to collect their offerings. Mrs Thornton's patchwork was beautiful and she admired it warmly.

"It ought to bring in a lot, especially the little cushions," she said, "they are so pretty and so much in request. I shall price them highly – it's a great mistake to let the nice things go too cheaply on these occasions."

Mrs Thornton felt flattered, for she valued Miss Bredon's praise. Mrs Perry wistfully delivered over two splendid white geraniums and a dwarf begonia and even more sadly two charming little streptocarchus. Miss Norton's distant cousin had responded quite generously; considering he was about the only relative she had left, he felt guiltily grateful to her for making so few demands on him and sent his annual box of foreign souvenirs (for he was a frequent traveller) with a good grace. Leila Ford suggested that what she called "my modest contribution", which was a large coverlet of knitted squares, would brighten up the stall if hung prominently in the front, "Not upon the stall, Miss Bredon, where it would be hidden and wasted, don't you think?"

Miss Brown apologetically said she had not been able to finish her crochet jacket in time, but it had been bespoke by the kind vicar for an old lady he knew, and would be paid for in advance. Honor guessed that more than half Leila's coverlet and all the dull matching and sewing together of its squares would have fallen to her lot.

Miss Hughes had been pleased when she was called upon to

take charge of the White Elephant Stall. She decided that she must have a new outfit for the occasion. It would not do to let The Haven down, especially as she was now a committee member. So she made a special trip to London to a little shop she knew just off Bond Street and bought a summer suit of an expensively subtle shade of lilac. She was lucky enough, too, to find a hat to go with it, a fine soft straw, not easy to get nowadays and really quite reasonable considering. She returned home well satisfied. But beyond that her imagination did not reach, so now, suitably dressed as she was to preside over her stall, she found it was empty except for a small hand-propelled mowing machine from the vicarage and a pair of hideous vases, a wedding present long ago to Mrs Bradshaw from an aunt, now deceased. Miss Hughes was unperturbed, she had not had any idea of what had been expected from her, nor had she now, but with the calm assurance induced by the cushioning of wealth, she assumed that all would be arranged satisfactorily somehow. As of course it was. A hasty round-up was called for; articles, however potentially unsaleable, could not be removed from other stalls without causing offence, but Col. Bradshaw took his car forthwith and set out for a house to house rally, thinking as he did so that he had almost given up Miss Hughes. He returned with an assortment which had mostly been intended for the Guides' jumble sale the following week. The White Elephant Stall, however, still looked rather thin on the ground, and then he and Mrs Martin, who had the next site for her produce, saw Tom lugging the old knife-cleaning machine across the lawn towards his ladies' stall. He was intercepted by Miss Blackett.

"Whatever are you doing, Tom?" she cried.

Tom grinned up at her joyfully. "This be for our ladies, Lady Miss Blackett. "I'm a-giving of it."

"What nonsense," said Miss Blackett, "It's not yours to give – besides no one will buy a thing like that – take it back to the house at once."

"It be from my room, Lady Miss Blackett, and so it be mine to do what I like with. Lady Mrs Thornton, she tell me so."

"You must have mistaken her − now take it away, there's a good boy, and go and help Mr Jackson put up the coconut shies."

"Wait a moment, Miss Blackett," called out Col. Bradshaw, "I believe Miss Hughes could do with it − it's a curiosity and might catch someone's fancy. We want a few more things here if you can spare it, that is."

"I can't believe it's worth the space it'll take up," said Miss Blackett, "but you're welcome to it," and she hurried off.

Tom was reluctant to deprive his ladies of his gift, but was persuaded that it was more likely to sell if in the company of the mowing machine than surrounded by pieces of embroidery and babies' woollies. He went off to help Mr Jackson, but in the course of the morning, the dressmaker's dummy, the chipped jug and basin, the volumes of *Sunday at Home*, the lampshade and the umbrella, all found their way to Miss Hughes's stall, where they certainly helped to fill up the gaps.

The sun was now at its height and it was very hot, everywhere but in Miss Dawson's room. She had decided to spend the day there. She had never liked parties and liked them even less now. It was pleasant to look down through the slats of the flat black branches of her tree and see everyone else running to and fro in the heat like frenzied ants.

"It's no use, Mary," she said to Mrs Perry who was trying to persuade her to come down for a little while later on and listen to the music, "I don't wish to come, and that's that. I've nothing against your grandchildren and you can come and tell me how wonderful they've been afterwards. Now, go along and enjoy yourself and leave me to do so quietly here in my own fashion."

Lord Jim was of Miss Dawson's way of thinking. As soon as

he realised that the usual civilized order of the day was to be upset by strangers and unseemly bustle, he decided to spend it in a sensible place immune from disturbance. He chose Tom's attic, and after inspecting the unfamiliar spaces left by the removal of the knife-cleaning machine and other articles, he settled down to a comfortable oblivion. It was fortunate that he had been out hunting the previous night and that a fat mouse had preceded his usual ample breakfast, so that it was unnecessary to bother about a midday meal.

At noon Lady Merivale, coming in from the garden where she had been lifting daffodil bulbs, found her husband in his study, which was a cool room, and sank gratefully into a chair.

"Do you think we should plant a border of narcissi along the west border this year?" she said.

After he had given the matter due thought and pronounced upon it (they were both keen gardeners), she remained there lying back with her head resting on the cushion. This was so unlike her usual habits that he was moved to ask her if anything was wrong.

"The heat's given me a headache and I was wishing I hadn't to go and open The Haven fête this afternoon, that's all."

"You drive yourself too hard sometimes, my dear. Wasn't it rather foolish to lift bulbs in this weather? We're not so young as we once were, you know."

"I suppose not; it's curious, isn't it, that now it does sometimes strike one that one isn't. I mean, for years and years one regards one's present state as static, and then suddenly old age looms up as a sea change in the not too distant future – and of course one tends to think of the old as static, too, I mean as if they have always been as they are now. It needs quite an effort of imagination to picture The Haven residents as young, for instance, or even as middle-aged like us. It wonder sometimes – don't you? – what we'll be like at their age, if we're still here at all, that is."

"No," said her husband, "the present's enough for me and a bit more than enough for you today it seems. You'd better go and have a bit of a rest before luncheon."

"Oh, I'm all right, and I don't need to stay long this afternoon, only make my little speech and do the rounds of the stalls, what are you doing?"

"I shall go to sleep," said her husband firmly, and with a sigh of envy she left him.

Lunch was served early at The Haven that day, but either owing to the heat or to the general excitement, no one but Leila Ford and Old Misery ate very much. Talking, on the other hand, flowed more easily than usual.

"How it livens us up when anything other than the daily routine is happening," thought Mrs Thornton.

Meg Norton, usually so silent, was speaking with some animation about the county cricket club results to Mrs Perry, and Leila was holding forth to the table at large upon a charity performance of *A Midsummer Night's Dream* given long ago in the grounds of Warwick Castle in which she had played Titania.

"Or wished you were playing her," silently commented Dorothy Brown, "you were really only one of the fairies."

"It was just before I left the stage for ever," said Leila. "Ben Greet happened to be in the audience and he congratulated me afterwards. He said I had a bright future before me, but, alas! I was infatuated at the time – my heart has always led me astray."

"It must have been a wonderful experience," said Mrs Thornton politely, "and what a lovely setting the grounds of Warwick Castle would have provided for The Dream."

"Indeed, yes!" said Leila. "I always feel that the spirit of the Bard haunts our Warwickshire in a very special way, don't you?"

Mrs Thornton gave an inward shudder. It is terrible when false tongues speak truth, or what one would like to think is true.

106

In the kitchen Old Misery was passing up her plate for second helps with relish. "Always partial to a bit o' fat, myself," she said, eyeing Gisela's plate, the rim of which was decorated with discarded bacon rind. "Waste not, want not, we was brought up on, not as 'ow that's always true neither. My mum, she never wasted a mite, but there was plenty o' want about all the same. It ain't 'alf 'ot now, reckon we'll 'ave a storm afore the day's out."

The musicians, having arrived early enough to rehearse Tom, were picnicking in the copse. They had found a sizeable oak to give them shade.

"He does love his drum," said Nell. "I thought he would. I wish he could keep it. It's a pity about his clothes."

Tom after all had not fitted at all well into the shirt and jeans she had brought along for him. He was shorter than Nell and a good deal broader, so the jeans had been far too long and tight and he couldn't squeeze himself into the T-shirt at all.

"Whatever made you think he was my size, Jake?"

"Oh," said Elizabeth, "all men are utterly hopeless about people's appearances, especially their clothes. If you ask them they say vaguely, 'Oh, he's not all that big,' or: 'Well, she was wearing a sort of blue thing.'"

"You're absolutely right," said Nell, "it was silly of me to trust to Jake. Tom's own clothes are pretty shabby, but it can't be helped now, *he* doesn't mind. Doesn't he hum beautifully? And he is so happy."

"I think we might borrow a begging-bowl from Gran and collect contributions for The Haven; every little helps, we'll just have it in front of us so people won't feel they've got to give," said Austen.

"This wood must be pretty old," said Jake, "look at that ancient thorn."

"Gran says there was an old farmhouse here, possibly Tudor, before The Haven was built. Tom's great-great-grandmother used to work there," said Nell.

"I expect the wood is older than that – reaching back to mediaeval times or further, some ancient boundary, perhaps."

"I wonder if Tom's ancestors planted any of it," said Nell. "I love the ancientness of it, it makes me feel bigger than I am, somehow."

"I should have thought it would have made you feel smaller," said Elizabeth. "I haven't much use for the past myself. We can't really progress unless we cut clear of tradition."

"Can't be done," said Austen, "and what d'you mean by progress, anyway? Cutting down this oak and the rest of the wood and building council flats here, I suppose?"

"Yes, if needed."

"Look," said Nell hastily, "there's Gisela and Tom going across the lawn to the marquee – their meal must be over – we'd better pack up and go and see if we can lend a hand."

She was right, the old ladies were all back in their own rooms getting ready for the afternoon. Dorothy Brown was trying to compress Leila into her best summer dress. Until recently the weather had been so unseasonable that she had had no occasion to wear it; it had been tight for her last summer and now was impossibly so.

"It's no use, Leila," said Dorothy, "it simply can't be done."

"You're not trying," Leila shouted, "it was perfectly all right when I last wore it."

"No, it wasn't," said Dorothy, "don't you remember, I had to let it out and now there's no more that I can let out."

"But what can I do?" wailed Leila. "I haven't anything else thin enough that's fit to be seen."

"We must use safety pins," said Dorothy. She disappeared into her own room and came back with two large safety pins which she fastened firmly where it was most necessary, and a skilful arrangement of a silk scarf hid the gaps through which Leila bulged.

"It isn't as if you'll be moving around," said Dorothy. "We'll go down early enough to get you a seat in the shade and there's absolutely no wind."

Leila continued to moan but Dorothy paid no attention. She found her increasing deafness actually an asset now in dealing with Leila – she need not hear what it was unnecessary to hear.

At 2.30 p.m. punctually, Lady Merivale declared the fête open, the young musicians struck up the "Toreador's Song" and people began to move round the stalls. Everywhere throughout the country can be found a band of splendid women whose unfailing contributions of homemade jams and marmalade, chutneys and sweets, cakes and flans appear at all the innumerable charity coffee morning, sales and fêtes. These faithful willing workers are taken for granted, but they provide an indispensable service to the community. Their goods disappear quickly, too, for they are always excellent value. Indeed, it is not unknown for the donors to buy back their own gifts themselves, at the fixed price, of course, rightly judging them to be of excellent quality. For instance, Mrs Martin, knowing exactly how many eggs and lemons had gone into her lemon curd, secured it for her married daughter, and there was always competition for Mrs Brewer's delicious fudge and Miss Anderson's coffee cake. Thus the produce stall had little or no difficulty in disposing of its wares. Friends and relatives saw to it that the old ladies' work also sold well. Mrs Thornton's patchwork was snapped up at once and so were Mrs Perry's plants. Lady Merivale, dutifully doing her rounds, bought Leila's coverlet, thinking it would do nicely for one of her "Help the Aged" parcels. She often managed to kill two birds with one stone in this fashion. She left the coverlet to be delivered to her later.

"Lady Merivale has such good taste," said Leila, as she

moved the SOLD ticket to a more prominent position. "Of course, she saw it would ruin the appearance of the whole stall if she took away my coverlet now – so thoughtful."

The White Elephant Stall was not doing so well. Miss Hughes sat between Mrs Bradshaw's great vases beaming with benevolence and handing out the wrong change to the few buyers who came her way. The vicar's wife, who was selling tea tickets nearby, looked with envy at Miss Hughes's beautiful outfit. She herself had not had a new summer dress for some time, in fact, now that her little girls were growing so fast and seemed to need new shoes at such short intervals, she got most of her clothes at the Oxfam shop in Darnley. She looked round now for Becky and Sue and saw them flitting about among the crowd, with their little trays of posies which they were very busy selling. The flowers were wilting already in the heat but everyone was buying them. "They can't resist the darlings," she thought fondly, "they look like flowers themselves; how pretty their frocks are – I'm so glad I chose those patterns and managed to finish them in time," and all envy of Miss Hughes melted away.

The musicians were hard at work and their begging bowl was filling up nicely. Down by the coconut shies, though, matters were not going too well. Bert Warren, the greengrocer's son, was too good a shot and was amassing coconuts with disconcerting speed. His father, still angry at Mr Jackson withdrawing his order, had forbidden Bert to go to the fête, but Bert did not mean to have his afternoon's sport spoiled; he could sell his coconuts at a profit at school the next day. But Jackson, seeing his stock disappearing too fast and all to the same customer, and that customer Bert, felt that this would cause trouble, and declared that from henceforth no one was to have more than three turns of three shots each. Bert, who was enjoying his sixth turn and had the ball in his hand, was annoyed by this and hurled it hard and recklessly in consequence. It flew through one of those neglected holes in the net straight at Lenny, Old Misery's youngest, for "old" was figurative rather than accurate and Lenny had only just turned six. He had drawn nearer and nearer the shies, fascinated by Bert's skill, and now loud shrieks rent the air, drowning the sweet strains of "Summer Dreams".

Lenny was borne off to the house – "All over bloo 'e is," said his sister Doreen with relish to the somewhat abashed Bert.

"It's knocked out two of his front teeth," said Mrs Mills later to an anxiously enquiring Mr Jackson at the kitchen door, "but the bleedin's mostly from his nose. Fred's putting a key down his back at this moment. The teeth were loose anyways, milk teeth they was, but it'll make his mother's day."

When most people had finished their tea, the draw for the raffle prizes took place. Sue, the vicar's younger little girl, tremendously solemn, picked the tickets from the brass bowl which usually stood in the hall, and handed them to Col. Bradshaw, who shouted numbers out through a megaphone. It had always been understood that should any of the committee or the donors of prizes draw a number they should hand back their ticket, but Miss Hughes had not grasped this, so when she was drawn she went up to choose her prize. By that time there were only the architect's drawing and her own clock left. She was pleased to get her clock back again – it had been inconvenient to let it go as she had intended it in the first place for her housekeeper's Christmas present. It was at this point that Col. Bradshaw finally gave her up.

And now it became noticeable that clouds were darkening the hitherto bright sky and that they looked remarkably like thunder clouds. It was extraordinary how rapidly they blotted out the blue; without further warning lightening flashed, a great clap of thunder sounded almost overhead, and a few large drops of rain splashed down. Immediately people began feverishly to pack up

111

what remained on the stalls and to hurry into the marquee, the rain then poured down in earnest and there was general confusion and dismay. Jim Bailey, the village postman who was a wit, seized the megaphone and shouted through it: "The rain is free, but we charge extra for the thunder." This made everyone laugh and feel better. The unsold goods were collected carefully in a corner and it was suggested that they should be auctioned. Mr Jackson, who had plenty of experience of auctions, was put in charge. There were not a great many articles, most were from Miss Hughes's stall, but of Tom's contributions only the knife-cleaner was left; the china and the volumes of *Sunday at Home* had gone quickly, Austen had bought the dressmaker's dummy, he said clothed or unclothed it would add distinction to his room, and Nell had got the lampshade for 10p. "The frame is sound and I shall cover it with parchment and some pressed leaves." What had happened to the umbrella was not known. Tom felt sorry for his knife machine. He went up to it and patted it.

"Don't often see one of them about nowadays," said Mr Martin to Austen, who was standing nearby. Mr Martin had arrived late from a meeting of the Darnley Preservation Society, and had not had time to go the rounds of the stalls before the storm.

"I suppose not," said Austen.

"Might catch the eye of an American," went on Mr Martin. "Edwardian relic, you know, quite the thing now. I'm a bit of a collector myself, not showpieces, can't afford them, just odd bits here and there, rubbish the wife calls them, but I find them quite an investment, you'd be surprised." Austen smiled at him and wandered away to find Jake.

The turn of the knife machine was not long in coming. "Now," shouted Jackson, "who'll be in luck and acquire this valuable piece of equipment, still in full working order – what

112

shall I start it at – say 50p.?"

Mr Martin put up his hand; he did not expect any competition but Jake, who was standing at the opening of the marquee watching the storm, turned and waved.

"That gentleman there," said Jackson. "Yes, sir?"

"One pound," said Jake.

"And fifty," said Mr Martin.

"Two pounds," said Jake.

"Three," said Mr Martin, whose desire for the knife machine was growing with competition. Everyone became interested, the bids steadily mounted, but at twelve pounds, Jake thought it wise to withdraw. The knife machine gave place to a stuffed owl that had lost half his feathers, but it had made by far the top price.

The storm had moved off, though it was still raining. Austen, Elizabeth, Jake and Nell slipped away as soon as the auction was over and set their faces towards Stratford. They had decided beforehand to make a night of it, and Jake had booked seats for the evening performance. They bundled into his car, which was larger than Austen's, and had an open top.

"Where are you going to put that thing?" said Elizabeth to Austen, who was clasping his dummy to his breast. "It won't go in the boot. Whatever possessed you to buy it?"

"Answer number one: I shall carry her on my lap. Answer number two: to please Tom."

"He did well, I must say," said Elizabeth. "What a pity he isn't at a special school, I'm sure they could teach him to read and write. Perhaps I could get him a place in one."

"That's right, shut him up in an institution. Will reading and writing make him any better off than he is already? He's free and useful and happy and himself as he is."

"All the same, I think people like him do need specialized care."

113

"What do you mean by 'people like him'? I don't see that Tom's any different from us except that he's got perfect pitch, which none of us have."

"Jake thinks he's different, don't you, Jake?" said Nell, teasing, but he did not answer. He was driving them through the lanes, avoiding the motorway, a habit of his that distressed Austen, who liked to get to places as quickly as possible. The rain had almost stopped and the air was deliciously fresh and cool.

"I feel just in the mood for Shakespeare," said Nell, "only not tragedy."

"It's all right, I think it's *Twelfth Night* or *Much Ado* tonight. I can't remember which," said Elizabeth.

"Neither," said Jake, "it's *The Tempest*."

"That's better still," said Austen, "that's got everything, men and gods."

"Gods?" queried Nell.

"Juno and Co.," said Austen.

"Every kind of magic," said Jake.

"And music," said Elizabeth. "Remember 'sounds and sweet airs that give delight and hurt not'?"

"Like we've been making," said Nell, "it's really got all today in it, old age and us."

"And Tom," said Jake.

Nell laughed at him again. "You and Tom," she teased.

"And it's got the wood with that oak tree," said Austen, "and the vicar's bees and Tom's bats."

They lapsed into silence. The lanes got narrower and turned about so that Jake had to go slowly and the branches of trees and bushes brushed against them. Summer scents invaded the car. The sky had cleared and a few stars were beginning to glimmer faintly in the dark.

"I'm so sleepy," said Elizabeth.

114

"Have a shoulder," said Austen. He disengaged an arm from his dummy and slipped it round her, drawing her gently towards him.

"Well, that's over," said Miss Blackett to herself as night fell and peace descended on The Haven once more. It had gone well on the whole, she thought; the storm had not really mattered and it had mean that the marquee had been most useful after all. She hated waste. The Lenny child had not been badly hurt, thank goodness it was only his nose and a couple of milk teeth and not his eye, but they must not use those nets another year without a careful mend. She hoped that they might have made a bit more than last year, the attendance had been good. Col. Bradshaw would let her know soon, she knew; he was very reliable. Her door opened gently and Tom appeared with Lord Jim. In spite of constant injunctions, he did not often remember to knock.

"He was on my bed, Lady Miss Blackett. I think he be hungry."

Lord Jim knew very well that he was, who wouldn't be after such a well spent day, slightly disturbed by the thunder, but on the whole, satisfactory. He rubbed against Miss Blackett's legs purring loudly in anticipation of his supper, which she immediately produced for him from his holy fridge. She did not thank Tom; she would have preferred Lord Jim to have sought sanctuary on her own bed, which he had always done before whenever the need arose. Tom stood there smiling.

"It's bin a grand day, Lady Miss Blackett, weren't they tunes lovely?"

"I hope you thanked Mr Perry for letting you join with his party, it was extremely kind of him, and Tom, I hope you are grateful for being allowed the time off to do so," said Miss Blackett.

"That little old drum fair played hisself, he did," said Tom and hopped out of the room.

"Such an irritating boy," thought Miss Blackett. "I do wish I could hear of a really reliable girl or woman instead."

9

SOME GOODBYES

A PERIOD of calm succeeded the fête. Mrs Nicholson, the new resident, moved in and seemed to Miss Blackett as though she was settling nicely and likely to give little trouble. Of course she brought too much furniture with her, they always did, but she was quiet and very cheerful. Her cheerfulness sprang from the fact that she looked upon the home as a real haven and not, like many of the past and present residents, as a depressing necessity. She had given up her own house some time before, owing to heart trouble. It was impossible to get enough domestic help and the garden had got beyond her long ago, so she had gone to live with a married son. But it had not answered. Not that they had been unkind to her, quite the reverse. Her daughter-in-law Carol was dreadfully kind.

"Bob and I have moved out of our room into the guest room, Mother; we thought you should have the sunny one. No, really, we *like* the room and it doesn't matter a bit not having a guest room. After all, blood's thicker than water, isn't it?"

"No, Kevin, you can't have 'Top of the Pops' on now, dear; I am sure Granny doesn't want it – no, Granny, please – he must learn to think of you before himself."

"Amanda, take your dressmaking things up to your bedroom, dear – no, it isn't too cold. Remember this is Granny's sitting-room now as well as your children's den, and you see you are taking up the whole table *and* most of the floor as well. Oh, Granny, if you insist, you spoil her, you know, but I'm sure she's very grateful."

"No, certainly you mustn't walk to your church, Mother. No. I'm afraid none of the neighbours do seem to go, it's rather shocking, isn't it, but Bob can easily run you there and call for you again later; he only potters about on Sunday mornings and he can fit those two short journeys in nicely." And Bob, who had been such a downright outspoken boy, now seemed unable to say anything but "Of course," though in all sorts of ways she felt she was unwillingly adding to the burden of his already too busy days. She could not have borne it had she not put her name down for The Haven, unknown to Carol and Bob. Perhaps if she could have gone to her daughter's it would have been different. "A son's a son till he gets him a wife, a daughter's a daughter all her life." Yes, but only as far as her circumstances will permit, and Peggy had her plate full, what with her job and three children and, she feared, a rather difficult and exacting husband, let alone that there really wasn't an inch to spare in their flat. So she had been overjoyed when she heard that there was a vacancy at The Haven and that she could move in at the end of August. Carol and Bob were hurt at her insistence on leaving but, all the same, she could almost feel the relief blowing through the whole household like a freshening breeze. Now, when they came to see her, which she was sure they would do, they could enjoy each other.

Mrs Nicholson liked the warden's brisk businesslike manner, she liked the little notices stuck up in her room about times of meals, baths, etc. How dreadful it had been when Carol had served the evening meal an hour earlier to suit her. She knew that it suited nobody else and it had even been changed from dinner to a light supper for her sake. ("I know it is much better for you, Granny dear, and I expect it is better for all of us, the

118

children get a good wholesome midday feed at school, and they do serve cooked dishes as well as sandwiches at Bob's office canteen.")

Then Miss Blackett told her that the vicar came regularly to celebrate Holy Communion for those who could not get to church. Depending on Bob and his car for her services on Sunday had worried her so much, as she knew how it cut into his one well-earned leisure morning, and yet they meant so much to her. She loved, too, the solidity of her room with its Victorian sash windows and handsome fireplace, though this of course was filled in now. It reminded her of the rooms she used to know in her childhood. Bob and Carol's house, with its open-style rooms and great picture windows, had hardly seemed like a house at all. The greater part of her furniture had been sold when she gave up her home, but a few precious pieces and pictures she had put in store as there was really no room for them at Carol and Bob's. Seeing them all round her again now was like a reunion with old friends. As she hung her carved wooden crucifix over her bed and her print of Raphael's Madonna over the mantelpiece where she had found two convenient nails, Mrs Nicholson gave "humble and hearty thanks for all God's goodness and loving-kindness" to her in bringing her to The Haven.

"That Mrs Nicholson, she is Catholic, I think," said Gisela to Tom. "She has a cross upon the wall and a picture of the Virgin and some lady saints painted on her bookcase also."

Miss Blackett overheard her. "You shouldn't gossip about the residents, Gisela," she said, "and in England such things do not necessarily mean that you are a Roman Catholic; you might well find them in our vicar's study, for instance."

Gisela sighed; here was another of those English muddles. In Germany, if you had crucifixes and Virgins and Saints in your room, you were Catholic, if you did not, you were good

119

Lutherans, like her parents.

Tom had not seen Mrs Nicholson's room yet. He was pleased that she had come; he did not like rooms to be empty. He decided it was time to pay her a call. Mrs Nicholson was sitting by a small round table which held her work basket and a row of well-worn devotional books between two painted bookends. They were rather poor reproductions of pre-Raphaelite ladies and not saints, as Gisela had supposed, but they held lilies in their hands and looked holy. Mrs Nicholson was knitting and thinking how lovely it was that no one was being kind to her any more, but she had reckoned without Tom. He, together with Lord Jim, who had also decided to call, entered the room without warning. Tom came forward for his handshake.

"You be the first new lady since I comes here," he announced.

Mrs Nicholson, though she had already heard something about him, was a little startled. She laid down her knitting to respond, her ball of wool rolled on to the floor and Lord Jim decided to put on a juvenile act. He pounced on the ball and rolled on his back, clasping it with his front paws. Tom crowed his funny laugh and Mrs Nicholson began to feel at ease. Tom tickled Lord Jim, who let go the ball to bite his fingers and pretend to claw him, and he retrieved it and rewound it neatly. Lord Jim turned his back on them and began an inspection of all Mrs Nicholson's furniture and Tom, too, began to look about him. He turned quickly away from the crucifix, but stared up intently at the Raphael Madonna.

"Are you thinking how beautiful that picture is?" asked Mrs Nicholson.

"No," said Tom, "I do be thinking he be a monster little 'un. I reckon as his Mum's arms must be aching summat terrible."

Mrs Nicholson was taken aback; she had never viewed her picture in this light before and there was no denying it, the divine Child was certainly rather large, but she was quite sure that

Tom was wrong about His mother. Raphael's Virgin had never felt weariness or strain; perhaps her arms were miraculously strengthened to bear the baby's weight. She suddenly realized that she was thinking of the picture as representing reality rather than the artist's vision. Did that matter? She thought it might. Ought she to explain to Tom that it wasn't like a photograph? But his attention had wandered to her two precious Ruskin pottery vases.

"Flowers," he was saying, "flowers for Lady Mrs Nicholson; which be your favourite flower?"

She could not think, it seemed a long time since anyone had asked her that sort of question really wanting to know the answer.

"I likes snapdragons," said Tom. "Vicar's bees, they get tricked by 'em sometimes, they be too heavy for 'em."

"Snapdragons, yes," said Mrs Nicholson gratefully, "such lovely colours."

Tom beamed and vanished, leaving the door open behind him, and Lord Jim, having satisfied himself that Mrs Nicholson's furniture was respectable and bore no traces of undesirable acquaintances, followed him. He was back again in no time with a big bunch of antirrhinums, orange and lemon and pink and crimson; there were plenty to fill the two vases. Mrs Nicholson did not ask where he had got them, though she did wonder about it a little, but he was so extremely pleased and happy she felt it must be all right. The flowers made the room look very bright and pretty, and when they had finished arranging them, they both surveyed the effect with satisfaction. Mrs Nicholson thought it perfect, only one thing worried her a little. The removal men had placed her chest of drawers across one corner, instead of flat against the wall. It looked better that way but she hadn't thought of the space it would leave behind which could not be reached and where dust would collect. She

121

found herself explaining this to Tom, who looked strong enough to shift it, which indeed he managed easily. Mrs Nicholson then opened the bottom drawer and took out a tin of fancy biscuits. She did not much like fancy biscuits but Carol thought that all old ladies did and bought it for the children to give their grandmother as a parting present.

"Thank you for helping me, Tom," said Mrs Nicholson, "and thank you for the flowers, it was very kind of you. Now, would you like one of these biscuits?"

"I be kind to you and now you be kind to me," Tom said, looking with pleasure at the biscuits, and Mrs Nicholson found that the distasteful word had somehow lost its sting.

Tom took a long while selecting his biscuit. At last he gravely chose out three and laid them before him on the table and then, after another pause, he replaced one of the three in the tin. Mrs Nicholson smiled at him as she used to smile at her small Bob.

"Keep both of those, if you like," she said, "and I'll have the one you put back to keep you company."

They ate together in silence and the fat Holy Babe looked down on them benevolently.

The weather had been so fine since the fête that harvest was over early and Col. Bradshaw delivered some of the spoils of Harvest Thanksgiving to The Haven for the old ladies in the first week in October. The scent of autumn was already in the air and some leaves were turned. Mrs Perry's border was a tangle of marigolds and larkspurs and dwarf dahlias. She did not care for the big showy ones, which were Fred's pride. "Like blowsy barmaids, I always think, though Austen tells me these don't exist any more, they are all university students earning a bit of extra money to pay for their cars, or even graduates, he says." She had had also a fine show of antirrhinums. She recognized them when she paid a welcoming call on Mrs Nicholson one day and guessed of course how they had got there. She did not mind,

122

there would be a second blooming and besides, she was happily looking forward to a visit to her eldest married granddaughter. Austen was fetching her for the christening of her third great-grandchild and she was staying on for at least a week.

The warden had decided that it would be a good thing to get the deodar tree cut down before the autumn damp set in. Mr Martin had supplied her with the name of a firm of tree surgeons and she wrote to them. After some time they phoned saying they would be round one day the following week. Miss Blackett sighed at the typical vagueness of the present day and she had further cause for sighing when the week passed without a sign. A return phone call produced regrets that, owing to unforeseen pressure of work, her job might have to be postponed until November. "How tiresome," thought Miss Blackett, "and they can't even say when in November." Then, without warning, the day after Mrs Perry had left for her visit, two men and a lorry with ladders, ropes and saws, turned up before breakfast and started to take off the top branches of the tree.

Miss Blackett had not felt it necessary to say anything to Miss Dawson about the tree coming down. She thought it better for the news to come as a nice surprise when the day for the felling had actually been fixed. Uncertainty of any kind always made old people fuss. Still, she certainly would have told her the night before had she herself known and, fearing that the old lady might, not unnaturally, be upset by the sight of a man suddenly appearing on a ladder or astride a branch close to her window, she thought she ought to go up to her at once.

Miss Dawson had been dozing after a broken night of arthritic pain – she fancied she was watching a native dance to the beat of drums when it changed to the rhythmic noise of sawing, and she was back in childhood and John, her grandfather's gardener, was cutting the hazels in the nutwalk. "Doesn't it hurt them, oh, doesn't it hurt?" "No, Miss Fanny, they'll shoot out again fast enough and twice as strong." But the sawing got louder and louder; John and the hazel trees vanished as she opened her eyes, yet the sawing still went on. She looked towards the window and saw the dark shape of a man impossibly silhouetted against the sky and heard the sudden snap and crash of a branch. At the same moment Miss Blackett knocked and came in without waiting for an answer.

"I'm afraid you may have been startled, Miss Dawson," she said. "I meant to tell you but the men arrived this morning quite without warning. The old deodar tree is coming down; the committee agreed with me, I am glad to say, that your room would be much brighter and warmer and drier without it, altogether healthier, you won't know yourself, your rheumatism will feel the benefit this winter, I'm sure."

Miss Dawson felt she was choking — she had to force the words out: "S'stop them, s'stop them," she stuttered, "they mustn't — they must stop, they must stop!"

"It's quite all right, Miss Dawson, you need not be frightened, they are skilled men who know their job — there is no danger that the tree will fall the wrong way or any of the branches come crashing through your window. It's all quite safe. They'll soon finish clearing the top part, they say, and they won't bring the machine saw for the main trunk till tomorrow, so just don't worry yourself. I'll pull your curtains across and Gisela will be here with your breakfast very soon."

She left the room and Miss Dawson turned her face to the wall, she knew she was defeated. She had fought authority several times in her life, and with some success, but now she knew without any doubt that it would be of no use. She was too old, too alone and too helpless, and it was too late. The sound of the sawing, malignant and relentless, filled the whole room.

After an aeon it stopped and she was able to think again. "What had the woman said — 'The committee agreed with *me*'."

124

It was her idea then, well, she should pay for it. If the murder could not be prevented, it could be revenged. Then her breakfast came in and afterwards the sawing began again.

The thought of revenge helped Miss Dawson to endure the horror of the next day, when the devilish petrol saw whined and screeched through the hours until her proud, beautiful tree crashed to the ground. She pondered long on what form this could take, but found nothing that satisfied her. All that time she never left her room.

Miss Blackett said, "Don't you find the noise disturbing? Why not stay downstairs in the sitting-room till they have finished?"

Miss Dawson did not answer. Miss Blackett found her silence a little disturbing, but Miss Dawson had always been a moody one, and really it was best not to worry too much about any of the old dears, but just to do what one knew to be right for them and, if she didn't mind the noise and preferred to stay upstairs, let her have her own way. It was certainly interesting to watch the men at work, she would have liked more time to see them herself.

It was on the day after the tree had fallen that Miss Dawson knew what was to be her revenge. Held prisoner by a sort of baleful spell, she had spent hours at the window watching the final stages of destruction. Lord Jim was equally, though very differently, fascinated. He had never experienced a horizontal tree before and much enjoyed stalking along it, sharpening his claws on its trunk, and pouncing on stray small twigs and dismembered branches. Frances Dawson looked down at his lithe golden body, so full of life, desecrating her dying tree, and hated him. Then it flashed upon her that of course her revenge on the warden must be to destroy her cat. It was so obvious and so just a solution that she wondered it had not occurred to her at once. She thought of the dead thrushes and the other poor

125

little corpses; this would be an act of revenge for them too. She remembered a talk with Mary Perry. She had said the only way to deal with cats was to get rid of them and Mary had said it would be difficult to get rid of Lord Jim, and she had answered, but not seriously, "Where there's a will, there's a way." Well, she was serious enough now, and a way must be found. She believed Mary was a little shocked at her then. She had been wishing that Mary had not been away during this dreadful time, for she alone would have guessed a little of what she was suffering. But now she thought it was just as well. She would certainly be of no help – too soft, and she might have proved a hindrance. "Where there's a will there's a way" – but what way?

Poison was the only possible answer, but how on earth was she to get hold of any? The problem occupied her all the rest of the day and by evening she was no nearer a solution, and she felt exhausted and frustrated by the time that the warden came in with her painkillers for the night. As her two regulation pills were shaken out, she stared at the bottle, because she did not want to look at Miss Blackett, and her eye caught the inscription at the base of the label. She did not have to read it, she knew it said: "Keep away from children and animals." That was it – that was the answer: hoard her pills, mix them with a tempting meal – fish, they always had fish for Friday suppers, that would do. Today was Tuesday, eight pills would surely be more than enough.

Miss Blackett said goodnight and left, and Frances grimly put away her pills. To forego her dose would mean long hours of pain, but she could endure more than that to achieve her end. During the next three days she kept a close watch on Lord Jim's movements. Like most cats, he was a creature of habit and addicted to a peaceful snooze after his meals. Since Tom's arrival he liked to take his morning nap on his bed, which smelt pleasantly of its owner and was safe from disturbance. Frances

Dawson noted that he passed her room on his way up to Tom's attic each morning at about the same time. On Friday evening she asked to have her supper served to her in her own room, a not unusual request with her. It was pilchards, and unluckily for Lord Jim, not in tomato sauce which he would not have touched, but pilchards in their natural state were exceedingly tasty. Frances pounded up her pills with the handle of a knife, mixed them with the pilchards on one of her own saucers and hid it in the bottom of her cupboard. She left a morsel of the fish on her tray.

"Miss Dawson, she has eaten nearly all her supper tonight," observed Gisela, "that is good, she has not eaten enough these days."

On that Saturday morning Frances, who had scarcely slept at all, struggled out of bed at the right moment, opened her door and put down the saucer of pilchards upon the threshold. Her fumbling arthritic fingers, shaking with excitement, nearly dropped it and she spilt some of the mixture, which worried her, but there was no time to clear it up. She sat down on the nearest chair and began to talk to herself.

"I'll have to take my chance of anyone noticing, but it isn't likely, they're all either in their rooms or busy downstairs now. If anyone does happen to pass, I'll say I wanted to give the cat a treat. I don't care what they think. I wish he'd come. The pills are almost tasteless, I know, and all cats are greedy."

Here she was wrong, all cats are not greedy any more than all people, but only an abnormal cat refuses fish. Lord Jim was not particularly greedy, but neither was he abnormal. This morning he was punctual as usual and was most agreeably surprised to find a saucer of pilchards on Miss Dawson's threshold. He cleared it up with relish and even attended to the spilt fragments. Then he went on his way rejoicing. Miss Dawson picked up the saucer and washed it thoroughly.

127

Miss Blackett missed Lord Jim first at his lunch hour. She was a little worried as his habits were usually so regular. When he did not turn up for his teatime saucer of milk she began to be anxious, but when he was still missing for his chief and most enjoyable meal of the day, the one he took after the residents' supper was over, she was seriously concerned. She went round asking everyone if they had seen him that day, but only Leila Ford remembered to have done so.

"I saw him early in the morning, Miss Blackett, he was going up to the attics, on his way to that boy's room I expect – he's always after him nowadays." Leila spoke with relish; she saw Miss Blackett's face harden into a stony mask and she sensed drama in the air.

Miss Blackett turned and marched upstairs; as she passed Miss Dawson's room the door opened slightly but she went on past it, straight on and up to Tom's attic. "He must have shut up Lord Jim there," she told herself angrily, "he would never have kept away from me for so long of his own free will."

She burst into the room. There was no Lord Jim there and no Tom either. She looked all round, on the bed and on the chair. But at a second glance the bed did not look quite right, there was a slight hump down the centre. Miss Blackett threw back the coverlet and revealed Lord Jim lying underneath. He looked far too shrunk and too still. She stood there motionless looking down at him.

Then Tom, who was coming to bed early as was usual with him, bounded past her with a queer cry and took up Lord Jim's limp body in his arms. Miss Blackett shrieked out at him:

"He's dead, you've killed him, its some hateful thing you've done like idiots do do to animals. He was quite, quite well – you've killed him, you wicked, wicked boy!" She rushed at him and struck at his head again and again.

"Stop that," said Miss Dawson's voice at the door. She had

heard the cries and had pulled herself up the stairs. "It wasn't Tom who killed your cat, I did."

Miss Blackett stared at her. "You!" she gasped. "You!"

"You killed my tree," said Miss Dawson, "so I killed your cat, a life for a life."

"But," said Miss Blackett, "a tree's not alive, not a *person*, I mean."

Miss Dawson simply looked at her, smiling a little. All of a sudden the silence between the two women was broken by sobs. Tom, still holding Lord Jim's lifeless body, had made no sound when Miss Blackett had attacked him, but now he burst out crying. His unrestrained tears, following each other down his cheeks, fell on the cat's fur which began to stick together as if he had been out in the rain. Miss Blackett snatched him from Tom's arms and put her face down against his wet coat. Immediately she was a child again, back on the night before her kitten had been taken away. He had jumped in at her bedroom window all wet and had leapt on to her bed and had dried himself by rubbing against her face, and this had tickled her so that she had laughed out loud in the dark. By the next night he had gone. Standing now with Lord Jim, so light and thin in her arms, she felt the darkness of destruction and loss envelop her. But also for the first and perhaps the only time in her life she experienced a moment of revelation. Looking up at Miss Dawson who was still calmly watching her, she suddenly seemed to see herself mirrored in the other woman's eyes. She and Miss Dawson were both, in some extraordinary way, one. She turned and went out of the room carrying the cat, and Tom followed her.

Miss Dawson dragged herself very slowly back downstairs in their wake. The unusual exertion and excitement had exhausted her and the consummation of her cherished revenge had left her empty. The pain, too, which she had had to endure while saving up her pills for Lord Jim, had taken its toll. She sat in her chair and stared out at the hateful open sky. After she had stared for a little while, she could not see the sky so clearly; there seemed to be branches stretching across it, and then more and more of them, waving softly as they used to do, and the room became full of bird song. Miss Dawson left her chair and flew through the window and up into the branches of her tree – up and up her bird's soul flew and at last, beyond all vision.

"I'm sorry, Tom," said Miss Blackett when they reached her room, "don't cry any more." She laid Lord Jim down on his cushion and got a clean handkerchief from a drawer and gave it to Tom – it was a specially large one that she kept for the specially heavy head colds from which she suffered. Then she sat down quickly. She was still trembling.

Tom blew his nose loudly, then his eye fell on Miss Blackett's teapot on the shelf. "Tea," he said, "tea for Lady Miss Blackett." He filled the electric kettle and switched it on and made the tea.

They drank it together without saying anything more, and afterwards Miss Blackett felt a little less shaky. Tom washed up the tea things, shook hands with Miss Blackett and stroked Lord Jim very gently and went off to bed. He woke at his usual early hour and got to work and, when it was time, went into the kitchen to set out the breakfast trays.

Gisela appeared and Tom shook hands with her and began to take the trays round. The ground-floor ones were done and he went upstairs with Miss Dawson's. Then Gisela heard him drop the tray – there was a crash and a sound of broken china, then she heard him run across the landing and, going to the door, she saw him sliding down the balustrade. He was laughing.

"She's gone, she's gone away, Lady Miss Dawson's gone," he shouted joyfully. "Come, Gisela, come Lady Miss Blackett, come and see."

Miss Blackett came slowly and heavily out of her room and followed Gisela upstairs. Gisela stopped outside Miss Dawson's room, afraid to go in, but Miss Blackett walked past her and Tom followed, still laughing. The breakfast tray lay on the floor with a broken cup and plate and the milk spilt all over the carpet. Miss Dawson's body was slumped forward in her chair. Miss Blackett could see at once what had happened.

"What a mess on the floor, they aren't supposed to die here, she's done it just for spite. This is my fault, I should never have left her to come down those stairs alone, I should have seen she was ill, it's my fault, I shall resign." All these thoughts shouted at her at once and she did not know what to do with them. But Tom's laughter, that had to be stopped immediately.

"Be quiet," she said sharply, "can't you see the poor old thing is dead? Be quiet at once."

10

TOM'S DEPARTURE

THERE WAS much for the warden to do that day – phone calls and interviews with the doctor, the undertaker, the vicar and Miss Dawson's "next of kin" (a cousin in Cornwall) and all the time she felt a heavy weight of oppression and weariness. It made things worse that her emotions were not clearly defined, but all mixed up and muddy. She could not find relief in anger against Miss Dawson, for she was dead, and the liberating moment of vision vouchsafed to her in the attic was already banished from her conscious thought. She had decided by now that Miss Dawson had been too ill to know what she was doing or saying.

She felt guilty at having accused Tom so harshly and violently, yet this did not prevent her still suffering from the jealousy that had occasioned the violence. It hurt that Lord Jim had died on Tom's bed, and that these last weeks he had seemed to prefer his company to her own. Then there was the question of how far she was responsible for Miss Dawson's collapse. She felt she ought to have noticed that she had not been eating properly for some days past and had been more than usually withdrawn; and, knowing how crippled and frail she was, should she not have seen her safely back to her own room? That she had not fallen on the stairs, seeing the state she was in that night, had been almost a miracle. Had she failed in her duty as warden and should she offer to resign? She felt it might be a relief to do so. These thoughts and emotions chased each other round her tired brain all that day, and underlying everything was the ache for Lord Jim, which she knew would be even worse when everything had settled down again.

She had no time to see to him before the late afternoon; then she found a good strong shoebox and lined it with a silk headscarf, a favourite one, and laid Lord Jim in it and, looking carefully to see that no one was about, she carried the box to the further side of the copse where the old thorn tree grew. Lord Jim had loved to climb that particular tree, it had a comfortable branch along which he liked to stretch out on hot summer days when Mrs Perry's border was too warm for him. Miss Blackett laid down the box while she went to fetch a spade. The ground was hard underneath the tree and she found it difficult to dig a big enough hole but she did not want to ask Fred to help her and certainly not Tom. At last it was finished, but she had been too tired to dig very deep and there was a mound which she tried to hide with moss and leaves. She did not want anyone but herself to know where Lord Jim was. When she got back to her room she felt utterly exhausted, but before she sat down to rest she put away Lord Jim's saucer and cushion where they could not be seen.

That evening everyone but Leila Ford was subdued for, though no one but Mrs Perry had known Miss Dawson at all well, the presence of death in the house made itself felt. The residents of The Haven were too old not to be aware of its inescapable reality, and its dark mystery, seeming now so close and intimate, blotted out their customary and comforting trivialities. Only Leila's rudimentary soul still believed that such a thing could never happen to *her*, and she was pleasantly roused and excited by the unusual drama of the day. Rumours were flying round about Lord Jim.

"Of course that boy is at the bottom of it. I saw the cat, you know, Dorothy, going up to his room yesterday morning. It was the last time he was seen alive. It was I who told Miss Blackett he was up there. No one else saw him, *and* I heard the row in the evening too. Mrs Thornton was with Miss Norton, *she* heard nothing. Well, what I say is that it only serves Miss Blackett right for employing such a boy here."

"You shouldn't say such a thing, Leila," said Dorothy Brown. "Miss Blackett says Lord Jim must have picked up some poison somewhere, probably rat poison, people aren't careful enough, and cats *will* wander."

"I wonder when Miss Dawson's funeral will be," said Leila. "I hope soon, I don't like the feeling of a corpse in the house. I hope we'll get somebody a bit livelier in her place. It'll make a change – she kept herself to herself, if anyone did. Funny, the tree and the cat and her all disappearing at once. My bottle's not hot enough, Dorothy; Gisela never does them properly."

"Give it to me," said Dorothy, "I'll heat it up for you."

After a night when she had slept from sheer exhaustion, Miss Blackett felt less inclined to offer her resignation. She decided to consult the vicar who was calling to see her about arrangement for the funeral service, she could not of course say anything about what had happened in Tom's attic, that was impossible, but she would try not to excuse herself in any way.

"I should have noticed that Miss Dawson had not been herself for some days," she began. "Gisela, our German girl, did say she was eating very little, but I did not take this seriously. Then, the night she died, for some reason she climbed the stairs to the attic floor. I should have prevented this, and certainly I should have seen that once there she should not have been left to come down those stairs alone, for I was aware that she was there. I ought to have seen that she was not fit to be left alone that night. In fact," she ended, "I feel I have been remiss and

134

that perhaps I should offer to resign."

"You are being too conscientious, if you don't mind my saying so, my dear Miss Blackett," exclaimed the vicar. "Miss Dawson was, I know, very reserved and she certainly did not invite questioning or sympathy. You must not blame yourself for what probably made no difference. After all she did *not* fall on the stairs. Perhaps the lack of appetite might have been a pointer, but it is easy to be wise after the event. I am quite sure the committee would not consider any offer of resignation from you for such a cause, and you must not think of such a thing. Now, about the funeral, don't let that worry you. I understand Miss Dawson left clear instructions that she wished to be cremated, and with no ceremony, but I think a short service at the cremation would be fitting, which I will arrange. Anyone who would care to be present from The Haven will be welcome of course —" he hesitated.

Miss Blackett said that she would like to come and Mrs Perry, if she were back in time, and she would enquire as to anyone else. She was relieved at the vicar's decisive reassurance. She really felt too old to start a new job and knew that she would not now easily obtain another post so good, and she could not afford to be unemployed.

"Goodbye, then," said the vicar, "and take care of yourself; you have had quite a shock, I can see. I shall send you along a pot of my honey, it is better than any tonic."

After Miss Blackett had thanked the vicar and seen him out, she felt her nagging sense of guilt partly assuaged, and more free to mourn her cat. Instinctively she found herself walking towards the copse, but when she got there she saw, to her dismay and indignation, that Tom was underneath the old thorn tree busily hammering away at some object on the ground, and that the little mound that covered Lord Jim had been carefully ringed round with roughly matching stones.

"What are you doing, Tom?" she asked.

Tom looked up. "I guessed as you might've laid him here, Lady Miss Blackett," he said. "The stones look right pretty, don't they? And I'm making him a cross all proper like, the wood it be from chips off that big old tree as is cut down."

Miss Blackett felt the usual uncomfortable conflict which Tom always seemed to arouse in her. She could not help being touched, yet she resented him thus trespassing on her private emotions, and as to the cross, that she considered really ought not to be allowed.

"Yes, the stones are nice," she said, "but not the cross, Tom, the vicar wouldn't like it."

"Oh, yes, Lady Miss Blackett," said Tom, "Vicar, he loves 'em, churchyard be full of 'em, and so be church."

Miss Blackett turned away. She knew that, in spite of anything she could say, the cross would be finished and if she removed it, another would be made to take its place. She supposed that now the little grave would be bound to be discovered and pointed out and talked about, and this she would hate, and yet, at the same time she felt an absurd childish gleam of comfort as if Tom's cross might ensure for Lord Jim a minute corner of heaven.

Mrs Perry managed to return to The Haven in time for Miss Dawson's funeral. She was very troubled and sad about her old friend's death. She alone guessed something of what the felling of the deodar tree must have meant to her. "Perhaps," she thought, "if I had not been away, I might have helped." It seemed heartless, too, that she had been enjoying her visit so much and especially her delicious new great-grandchild while this was happening to Frances. She sincerely grieved, too, for Miss Blackett's loss of Lord Jim, and she could not entirely suppress a very unwelcome query as to his death, which she would not put into words, even to herself. It was just there, like a little cloud which would not go away – but no, she simply would not think about it any more, it would have been impossible anyway. But perhaps this made her express her sympathy with the warden more openly and warmly than anybody else had dared to do in the face of grim discouragement.

"Dear Miss Blackett," she said, "we had a retriever once who was such a darling, he was a most beloved member of the family. He got run over. I know what it feels like, one misses such a pet at every turn – you must get another cat, it's the only way. We got a puppy directly. Of course it wasn't the same as dear Rab, but it healed and helped. My daughter's tabby has lovely kittens and I'm sure she would gladly give you one."

Miss Blackett felt her lonely unhappiness melt a little, but she shook her head. She was not going to lay herself open to the perilous arrow of love a third time. "No, thank you, Mrs Perry, I don't mean ever to have another cat, but I appreciate your kindness all the same."

Mrs Perry missed Frances Dawson very much. She had admired her for her courage and her knowledge, though she was always a little in awe of her. Now she began to cultivate Mrs Nicholson's company; it was Tom's raids on her flower border that first brought them together. He kept Mrs Nicholson's vases regularly supplied with snapdragons, which were now enjoying their second flowering, and when she learned that the only border where they grew belonged to Mrs Perry, she thought an apology was called for. But Mrs Perry just laughed.

"You're welcome," she said, "and nobody really minds what Tom does, bless him."

A bit later she wrote to Nell: "I find that our new resident, Mrs Nicholson, plays Scrabble well and we have a game together most evenings. We are about equal. She is a pleasant person, though very religious. She had an uncle who was a bishop, but this doesn't matter for Scrabble. Tom has made a cross for poor Lord Jim's grave and she thinks this is sacrilegious, I fear, but, as you know, I always say I shan't be happy in heaven if dear Rab isn't there, and really, I think that dolphins and seals and whales and poor dear gorillas and some, though not all, dogs and cats, have much nicer natures and are better behaved than many humans, and I shouldn't wonder if God doesn' think so too, so we'd better look out. But of course I can't say that to a bishop's niece. It is nice to have another grandmother here, poor Mrs Thornton has no grandchildren, you know – though I can tell that Mrs Nicholson's are nothing like so nice or clever as mine. Your loving Gran."

The evenings were now definitely drawing in, as the residents remarked to each other, and an early frost had blackened the giant dahlias, though Mrs Perry's little ones in their warm bed were still unscathed, when Miss Blackett received a letter from Mrs Bradshaw. It said that her own invaluable "help" possessed a lately widowed and childless sister who was anxious to find work and a home near herself. "She sounds a treasure and I thought of you at once, for I was sorry to hear from the vicar you had had the shock of the sudden death of one of your charges lately, and I am glad to think that more adequate help than the boy, whom you kindly took in as a stopgap, may now be available. She is giving up her home but would like to keep some of her furniture, and I hope it may be possible for her to have a room for herself and that she can make it into a bedsitter. If all goes smoothly, she should be free in two or three weeks' time."

Miss Blackett immediately determined that nothing should prevent her acquiring this treasure. Mrs Thornton really must now see the necessity of moving down to Mrs Langley or Miss Dawson's room – there was already another applicant but Mrs Thornton could take her choice first, leaving the big attic, so unsuitable for her but just right as a bedsitter for a resident help.

As for Tom, she could not pretend that it would not be a relief to get rid of him. He was a good little worker, but his behaviour was so unpredictable, so unreliable that sometimes, she admitted to herself, it thoroughly upset her. It had always been understood that his job was a temporary one, and she was willing to give him a good reference. She wrote a grateful letter to Mrs Bradshaw and resolved to tackle Mrs Thornton as soon as possible.

Fate played into her hands for once. Mrs Thornton stumbled on the stairs on the way down from her attic one evening and fell. She did not break any bones, but she was badly bruised and shaken. Miss Blackett took the opportunity to press home the advantage of a room accessible by the lift and which would be warmer in the coming winter months. Stairs were apt to be dangerous after a certain age, well, she had proved that already, hadn't she? Then she told her about "the Treasure" who must have a room of her own for a bed-sitting-room. Mrs Thornton lay and listened with an aching head and bones, and the fight went out of her. It would be selfish, too, she thought, to cling to her attic in the circumstances. She agreed to move as soon as she had recovered from her fall and she chose Mrs Langley's room, perhaps she would feel her gentle, merry spirit lingering there.

Next Miss Blackett summoned Tom to her. "Tom," she said, "you know when you came first, you were told it would probably only be for the summer, as I always intended to find someone older and more experienced when I could. Well, now I have found someone. She is a widow lady who wants a home, and she is coming quite soon, but you can stay your month out. You have been a good boy on the whole and worked well, and you can tell your grandmother I said so."

"He can make himself useful till Mrs Smith settles in," she thought.

139

Tom showed neither dismay nor pleasure at the news. He looked at her with his wide impersonal stare and said nothing. He could stand still and silent sometimes for quite long periods, as an animal will do, without any need to make himself felt, yet felt he inescapably always was.

"Do you understand what I am saying, Tom?" said Miss Blackett sharply.

"Farmer Jackson's Clover, she calved last night, Lady Miss Blackett, 'tis a fine little heifer, as like Clover as can be," said Tom, and went out of the room.

Everyone except Miss Blackett and Leila Ford were sorry to hear that Tom was going. "But he doesn't seem to mind at all," said Miss Brown to Mrs Thornton, "I don't understand it, he has always seemed so fond of us and so happy."

"I think it's just because he doesn't look before and after and pine for what is not."

Dorothy Brown looked blank. She had taken to a hearing aid but it was not always very helpful.

"I mean," said Mrs Thornton hastily, "that he just lives in the present moment. When it comes to the point I expect he'll show he's sorry; but I shouldn't count on it. He probably just accepts that things happen to him, some of them good, some of them bad, and that's that, as we used to do, didn't we, when we were children?"

"Did we?" said Dorothy vaguely. "Well, anyway, I was wondering if we could give Tom a parting present before he goes. It's nice when one leaves a job to be given a present, don't you think?"

"What a good idea," said Mrs Thornton warmly. "Had you thought of anything in particular?"

"I wondered if a new pullover might be welcome," said Dorothy, "the weather's getting colder and he's still got only his old patched thin one."

140

Miss Brown's proposal caught on; the pullover, a nice bright green one, was bought at Darnley's wool shop, and The Haven's champion knitters, Mrs Perry and Mrs Nicholson, worked hard at producing a pair of socks and a scarf to go with it. In the end everyone except Leila contributed towards a whole new outfit. Miss Blackett's feelings were again confused. She could hardly do less than fall in with the old ladies' charitable plan, she thought, nor did she grudge Tom the clothes exactly, but she felt too much fuss was being made of the boy. She decided it would be best to give the things to him as quietly as possible, and although he was staying on till the end of the month, to give them before the Treasure arrived. So, the evening before this arrival, which she was keenly anticipating, Miss Blackett called Tom into the sitting-room after supper where the ladies were all assembled and where, laid out on the table, were the pullover, socks, scarf and, besides, a pair of stout jeans and some strong shoes, also a large glaring check handkerchief contributed by Gisela.

Mrs Thornton was feeling a little nervous. It occurred to her that Tom might resent being given clothes. She wished it had been a drum, yet it was certain that he needed them.

"Tom," said Mrs Blackett, "the ladies and I are giving you a present, or rather several presents, because you are to leave us soon and you have done your work here well. I hope you will take care of these nice clothes, for you are a very lucky boy to have them given to you, you know."

"Oh, dear," thought Mrs Thornton, "why need she have put it like that? And she sounds as if she were scolding him instead of giving him a present, yet I know that it was she who bought him these very good shoes."

Tom simply stood and stared – motionless he stood, and Mrs Thornton held her breath until at last he stretched out a hand and very gently touched the soft wool of the jersey, but otherwise he still did not move or speak.

"Go off and put them on and let us see you in them," said Mrs Perry, and gave him a little push.

At that he hooted with delight, gathered up everything and bounded out of the room. Mrs Thornton gave a sigh of relief.

"He might have said 'Thank you'," said Miss Blackett.

"Oh, he will," said Mrs Perry, "dear Miss Blackett, he was so excited – that was really his thank you."

When he came back, it was seen to the ladies' satisfaction that the clothes fitted well. He had tied the scarf crossways over his chest and knotted Gisela's hideous handkerchief round his neck. He moved as in a trance and, going up to Mrs Thornton, took her by the hand and led her to the old piano. She thought she knew what it was that he wanted and, after a little hesitation, she struck up the opening bars of the Mazurka from *The Gondoliers*.

And then Tom began to dance round the room, lifting his feet in their new shoes high in the air, clumsily but always in time. At this point Leila Ford got up noisily and stumped over to the television.

"It's time for 'Dallas'," she said loudly, and switched on, not waiting for the warden's permission.

Miss Blackett, however, took no notice of this infringement of her rules. She felt she had had enough of the evening, and of Tom in particular, and, leaving the room, she sought the solitude of her office and shut the door upon everyone and everything.

In the sitting-room the double entertainment continued – Leila squatting huge and central before the horrific goings on across the ocean, and Tom, wrapt in his grotesque yet somehow rather beautiful dance, circling round her. The idea suddenly occurred to Mrs Thornton that he and Leila were the only two completely unselfconscious people in the room, and that this constituted a sort of bond between them. Leila, with her dreadful

142

perverted innocence, was a caricature of Tom. This thought disturbed her and she brought the dance to an end with a final chord, and closed the piano.

Then Tom shook hands twice all round, except of course for Leila who, ignoring him, continued to glare at "Dallas". When he came to Gisela she said wistfully:

"The handkerchief, it is from me, is it not very, very pretty?"

"It be *lovely*!" said Tom with great feeling. It was the first time he had spoken and Gisela felt satisfied. He turned towards the door and Mrs Thornton got up to go with him, but he rushed away without waiting for her, and she just caught a vanishing sight of him doing a handturn on the landing. It was the last she saw of him, for in the morning he was nowhere to be found.

Miss Blackett was angry. That Tom should take it into his head to disappear when he was still needed and after having had such kindness shown him appeared to her to be thoughtless, ungrateful and again most unreliable behaviour. She was not placated by Mrs Perry who said: "He'll have run home to show his Granny his new clothes, he'll be back before very long, I'm certain." She was right in the first supposition but not in the second.

As the day wore on and no Tom appeared, Miss Blackett grew angrier – Mrs Smith, the Treasure, was due to arrive in the late afternoon and the warden resented the fuss and distraction Tom's absence was causing.

Gisela was in tears. "That poor Tom," she cried, "he will have been over run and killed in the road, I think!"

"Nonsense, Gisela," said Miss Blackett, "stop being so foolish, if an accident had happened, we should have heard about it from the police." But she rang up the vicar and explained the situation.

"I am so sorry to trouble you, Vicar, but I think we should know what has happened to the boy, and I have no one else to turn to. We think he has most probably run home. If so, perhaps you could make him see how irresponsibly he has behaved and that unless he comes back at once and apologizes, it may affect the reference I can give him – that is, of course, if you should have any time to spare and can get over to Sturton."

The vicar, who still felt some responsibility for Tom, promised to investigate. He himself had no doubt but that Tom had gone home; as to the efficacy of Miss Blackett's threats and reproaches, he was much more doubtful. He found old Mrs Hobb sitting close to her little log fire with her hands, usually so busy, folded placidly in her lap.

Yes, Tom had come home, but was now off again on an errand for herself, she informed him quietly. She offered no further details.

"But he should not have run off like that, Mrs Hobb, Miss Blackett is very cross about it. He has caused anxiety and everyone is so surprised that he should have disappeared without warning and without saying goodbye. He was supposed to be staying the month out, you know."

"I be sorry, sir, that the lady be put out, but 'tis a wonder to me that it should be so. Tom said as there was a party and music and handshaking and, beyond all, those good new clothes as a present for his leaving, and so, to be sure, he left."

There was a little silence, then the vicar said, "I see."

He felt he could not give Miss Blackett's message as she had worded it, but that it was only fair to suggest that Tom should come back for the stipulated time.

"Maybe yes, maybe no," said the old woman. "'Twas a saying when I was young that 'fine clothes foretell a flitting' – Tom had the fine clothes and the flitting's done, and happen can't be undone and, sir, I be thinking I be for a flitting myself soon, it'll be further afield than the lad's and the fine clothes for it be laid ready in the press yonder."

144

She looked up at the vicar and saw that he knew what she meant.

"I'll be glad to have Tom by me till the time comes for it won't be long now, but if the lady *truly* wants him, maybe he'll go."

"She seemed to know quite simply and certainly that death was coming to her and when it would come," said the vicar afterwards to his wife, "and I believed her, and I wish you could have heard the way she said, 'If the lady *truly* wanted him.' I couldn't really convey it to Miss Blackett, though I tried."

But the warden would only have Tom back on her own terms, and he did not come. She felt justifiably aggrieved, and resolved to think no more of him. Yet an aggravating wish to see him once again persisted, a sense of something unresolved that might have been straightened out to some unspecified advantage — though whether to him or to herself, was not clear. She put away such muddled unprofitable feelings, but in the days to come caught herself thinking of the boy with a sort of dull regret.

Tom's unconventional departure was viewed wistfully by Mrs Perry, Mrs Nicholson and Dorothy Brown, emotionally by Gisela and pleasurably by Leila. Mrs Thornton, thinking it all over, with the memory of his dance and that last handstand on the landing, acknowledged to herself that she was not at all astonished.

"There was nothing ordinary about Tom," she said to Meg Norton.

"No," assented Meg, "and yet nothing extraordinary either, he always reminded me of a character out of one of our plays." Mrs Thornton thought that Meg often said rather surprising things.

" 'My gentle Puck,' are you thinking of him?"

"Oh, no, not Puck," Meg said and said no more. She had never told anyone of the time when Tom had rescued her from despair down by the copse.

"A mixture of Puck and Ariel, perhaps, together with a bit of one of the clowns or rustics to humanize him," laughed Mrs Thornton. "Anyway, a timeless natural being and therefore you're right, Meg — certainly to be found in Shakespeare, though, now I come to think of it, considering how he left us, I can't help remembering the tales my old nurse used to tell me about Brownies —

'Brownie has got a cowl and coat
And never more will work a jot.'

I wonder what will become of him."

"He'll be all right," said Meg with conviction, "we need not worry about Tom, but I shall miss him."

"I think we all shall in our different ways," said Mrs Thornton.

11

MRS THORNTON'S DREAM

MRS SMITH, the Treasure, was a small wisp of a woman with quick mouselike movements. She was everything that Tom had not been, completely predictable and amenable and anxious to do what was required, and Miss Blackett told herself that she was very pleased with her. She had, it must be admitted, one annoying habit. When spoken to she almost always repeated the last few words of the speaker like an irritating echo.

"I would like you to go to Darnley this morning to do the shopping."

"To do the shopping."

"You will remember that Miss Brown is decidedly deaf."

"Decidedly deaf."

This habit proved a barrier to any prolonged conversation and, besides, Mrs Smith was always on the move. If asked to sit down she was the sort of person who always sits on the edge of her chair, ready to pop off again. But undoubtedly she was a treasure and seemed only too eager to be ordered about by everyone from the warden downwards.

"That Mrs Smith, she is no better than a commuter," remarked Gisela gloomily to Mrs Perry who looked puzzled.

"What do you mean, Gisela?" she asked.

"You put in the words – so, and out come they again – so, and always she does what she is told."

147

"Oh, you mean a computer," said Mrs Perry, "well, computers are very useful, but I see they may not be very good company."

"Me, I am not staying," said Gisela, "now that I know my English so well, I go home. I go perhaps before Christmas comes."

"Oh, dear!" said Mrs Perry. "That is some time before your year is up, do stay with us until the spring."

"Yes, yes, I go, Mrs Perry, it was OK while Tom was here, but with a commuter – NO."

The successor to Miss Dawson's room arrived soon after Mrs Smith. Miss Long was a protégé of Mr Martin's. She was only in her early seventies, a retired secretary and still active and there seemed no very good reason why she should have come to The Haven. Miss Blackett privately thought that it was because Mr Martin found it convenient to have her there since she sometimes helped him out when he was particularly busy. Indeed she was seldom actually in the Home for she appeared to have many acquaintances in the district and she was inclined to adopt a patronising air towards the other residents. Mrs Thornton had hopes of her at first, for she noticed a row of rather beautifully bound volumes of poetry on a shelf in her room. But Miss Long, seeing her eyeing them, laughed and pulled one out. It was merely a box with the lid made to open like a book cover.

"My last employer gave them to me when he took up a post abroad, for he knew I had always admired them. He used them like files; bills went into Browning, circulars into Chaucer, letters into Longfellow, and so on. I do the same and I find it most convenient."

Mrs Thornton went away intrigued but sorrowful.

Even St Luke's little summer was now over, the leaves were still mostly thick on the trees but autumn colours were rife. The first autumn gale had blown down Lord Jim's cross – the ground had been too hard for Tom to have fixed it in securely. Miss Blackett let it lie and soon the little yellow leaves from the thorn tree would cover it up.

"The warden seems to have aged lately, don't you think?" remarked Lady Merivale to Miss Bredon after the autumn committee meeting was over. "Really she looks older than some of her charges, certainly than Mrs Perry."

"Shrivelled up, rather than old," said Honor Bredon. "You'd have thought that now she has Mrs Smith to take a good share of the work off her shoulders, it would have been the opposite."

The same thought struck Dorothy Brown one evening. She had lately managed it that if there was a travel film on television she would cajole Leila into going to bed early, never actually a very difficult task. Then she would slip downstairs again to enjoy herself. This particular evening there was a lovely film about Petra, "the rose red city", and she had it to herself which she preferred, for then she could think herself right into the scenes before her without disturbing interruptions. She had discovered – alas, far too late – what she would have liked to have done with her life. She would have been a traveller, even perhaps an explorer or an archaeologist, for she gloried especially in the ruins of ancient cities. She secretly collected select travel brochures over which she pored with a wistful pleasure. She was lost in excitement over this film when Miss Blackett came in at the regulation time to turn it off. Luckily it was just about to finish. There was something about the way the warden plodded across the room, not even noticing that Dorothy was there, that caught her attention. On a sudden impulse, for she always had been and still was an impulsive creature, Dorothy Brown said:

"I've been watching such a wonderful travel film, Miss Blackett, don't you ever want to go abroad? I'm sure you deserve a good holiday, and now that Mrs Smith has come, once she is thoroughly settled in, couldn't you take one?" She really

149

felt full of pleasure at the idea. "Do, do think about it," she added.

Miss Blackett was quite startled. "How very odd of Miss Brown to spring this upon me so eagerly," she thought. "Could she want to get rid of me for any reason?" The suggestion that The Haven could get on perfectly well without her she found particularly displeasing.

"It's quite out of the question, Miss Brown," she said, "besides I've never liked foreign places." Actually she had never been out of England except for a day trip across the Channel years ago.

"But their faces are so interesting," said Dorothy, "so different from ours, at least they were in Greece, I remember."

"I said *places* not *faces*," shouted Miss Blackett.

Really, it was too tiring to have to talk to Miss Brown at the end of a long day. But Dorothy continued, for she could hardly bear it that anyone who could travel should not do so. "I'm sure it could be managed," she said, "why not just send for some brochures – there are marvellous tours to be had nowadays and really quite reasonable." But Miss Blackett shook her head and left the room, shutting the door behind her with what was almost a slam, so that Dorothy felt the vibrations, which affected her disagreeably. She sighed with pity. This vehement negation of a possible joy depressed her.

As for Miss Blackett, the gust of annoyance aroused by Dorothy Brown's proposal soon died down. She dismissed her suggestion as she had dismissed the memory of Miss Dawson, Mrs Perry's offer of a kitten and any further encounter with Tom. She thought instead that it was time to prepare for winter and winter at The Haven presented problems, as to how to keep the old ladies warm and the bills down, with lofty Victorian rooms built for large coal fires, long passages, wide landings and outside pipes that easily froze.

"Don't forget to put your watches back," she announced on the last Saturday in October. "Christmas will be here before we know where we are."

"Before we know where we are," echoed Mrs Smith. Gisela snorted. She knew where *she* would be by Christmas.

The announcement was received gloomily by all the ladies except Leila and Mrs Nicholson. Leila alone welcomed an extra hour of night and the difference between summer and winter really meant little to her now – she could sleep and eat during both, but perhaps rather more so when the days were short and cold. But the others disliked the prospect of the long dark evenings and penetrating winds and damp, and cruel frosts and snow. Only Mrs Nicholson did not really mind much, for the prospect of winter at The Haven had its compensations. She could go to bed early if she liked, with her lovely hot water bottle and her books. Carol and Bob had given her an electric blanket, of which she was much afraid, and had said: "Now, Granny, you'll be beautifully warm all over and you won't need a bottle, in fact it's not quite safe to have one with the blanket." But you can't cuddle a blanket. And now she could read as late as she liked without Carol bustling in with exclamations and offers of a hot drink. She usually had two books on hand, a good story and a holy book, that was besides her Bible, of course. Nevil Shute, Georgette Heyer and Monica Dickens were among her favourite storytellers. But she was always faced with a dilemma. If she left her Bible reading and her holy book to the last, she was apt to fall asleep over them, yet, on the other hand, to end the day with a novel did not seem either quite reverent or comfortable. This night, which was a little solemn because it was the last night of summer time, she read her story first, but resolutely laid it aside before she had even begun to feel drowsy.

Mrs Perry had been planting her bulb bowls that day and now, before she went to bed, she patted down the fibre once again lovingly. "Sleep well for the next two or three weeks," she said to them, "and then get on with your growing." She did not like to think of the cold damp weather ahead, for she knew it was certain to bring her those tiresome bronchial attacks which got a little worse every year and, unlike her bulbs, she could not at her age look forward to much of a renewal of life in the spring. But, she told herself, the less she thought about that the better, and she was planning a winter knitting marathon for her family.

Mrs Thornton had by now reached *The Tempest* in her Shakespeare reading to Meg Norton and, like Austen, Elizabeth, Nell and Jake, she was filled anew with amazement at its all-embracing richness. She had just read Prospero's most famous speech and paused to look up and share the wonder of it with her friend, but saw that she was asleep. She looked frailer and older when her eyes were shut. There was no colour in her face, and this emphasized the still beautiful bone structure. She looked like a carved figure on a tomb, and at the thought Mrs Thornton felt a sudden pang. Mrs Langley and Miss Dawson had gone from their little company so recently – was Meg to be the next? "We are such stuff as dreams are made on, And our little life is rounded with a sleep." She repeated the lines to herself but the lovely words had lost their power to please. They now seemed menacing and dreary and she closed the book and gently left the room.

Behind her own door a deep depression engulfed her. She made no effort tonight to count her blessings. She did not feel at home yet in Mrs Langley's room but missed her attic with its sense of seclusion, and yet with the pleasant feeling of Tom just across the landing. Yes, she missed Tom curiously much and pervasively. Here, in this room, she was not immune from Mrs Nicholson's radio next door, and their tastes did not coincide. She could even hear Miss Brown's too, for this was always turned up loudly because of her deafness, and Mrs Thornton did not like to complain. Not that this was distracting her now, for both radios were silent as it was growing very late, yet she did not feel in the least like bed. She looked from the window after a little while and saw that Meg's light had been extinguished. Had it not been, she would have gone to her again. She felt anxious about her, or rather she supposed it was for herself, as if death should come to Meg soon she knew that she would not grieve for *her* as she was almost sure that she would welcome it. No, it was for herself she feared. She could not afford to lose Meg whom she had come to love. The years had robbed her of too much. It seemed another life, a different, incredibly rich world in which she had once lived among so many friends and, above all, where she had been supported and enlivened day in, day out, by the love, companionship and need of her husband. Compared to that lost solid world, existence at The Haven was poverty-stricken and flickering – here, where this little group of premature ghosts shuffled round waiting for the end. There was no comfort at all in the realisation that this slow dissolution was natural and to be expected by the majority. What sentimental rubbish was sometimes talked about old age – at its best it could only be called a bad job.

She had been standing by the window where she had gone to look for Meg's light and now she turned away but without drawing the curtain. A chill late autumnal fog had risen and it seemed so in tune with her present mood that she almost welcomed it. She switched on the radio for the World Service to distract her thoughts, but this only made her fearful and miserable on a wider scale. She had longed for children once, but now she felt glad she had no close personal ties with the future. She often wondered how people like Mrs Perry and Mrs Nicholson, with grandchildren, were not more anxious and alarmed at what appeared to be in store for them. But she

153

supposed that the temperamental optimism of the one and the simple faith of the other supported them. Mrs Thornton, who possessed neither, gave herself up to black despondency. She began to get ready for bed.

By now everyone else was asleep and it must be confessed that the inhabitants of The Haven did not look their best at such a time. Had one been able to see them, only Meg Norton and Mrss Perry could have been viewed with pleasure. Meg, in her spotless plain white nightgown, lying very straight and still beneath a similarly spotless white coverlet, was more than ever like a medieval effigy. Mrs Perry, propped up with fat pillows to help her breathe more easily, was comely still, her cheeks faintly tinged with pink that matched her fluffy bedjacket. Leila Ford had replaced her wig with a mustard-coloured knitted cap, which had slipped sideways, exposing part of her shining bald pate. She lay on her back and snored with her thick lips hanging loosely open revealing two or three old fangs of teeth. Her skin was wrinkled, leathery and grey, from the constant application of heavy make-up. She looked grotesquely ugly and pitiful, like some mythical monster.

Dorothy Brown next door was smiling in her sleep, the frowning strain of deafness gone from her neat pale face. Actually she was wandering among great red cliffs beneath a brilliant sky. Her thin grey hair lay across her flat chest in a childish plait, her cheeks were hollow and, with her teeth removed, her mouth was pinched and sunk. No one would have guessed that she was, almost every night, engaged in intrepid exploration.

Mrs Nicholson, too, appeared older now that look of placid content that beamed out from behind her spectacles during the day was absent. Her face had a bluish tinge and her breathing was a little uneven, but she seemed comfortable nonetheless, clasping her beloved bottle to her and with her shoulders snuggled into a beautiful lacy shawl knitted by herself.

Night had breached the brisk anonymity of Miss Long. She had taken from the book box named "Pope" a photograph of a handsome middle-aged man, her one-time employer — the one who had bequeathed her the boxes. This she had slipped beneath her pillow as was her wont. He would have been surprised to know that she frequently slept in his arms.

Mrs Smith had moved her bed out of the turret alcove, which to her had appeared spooky. Truth to tell, though she would never tell it, she found the attic room with no one near a bit frightening altogether. Her bed was now pushed against the wall furthest from the turret and she lay in it curled up tightly. Every now and then she twitched in her sleep. Tucked into the small of her back was a very old hairless Teddy Bear.

While all the ladies looked more ancient in sleep, Gisela looked younger. She sprawled across the mattress, abandoning herself to the deep motionless oblivion of youth. The fair hair which Tom admired so much strayed all about the pillow — one arm was flung across the coverlet; emerging from a flounce of bright red and green cotton sleeve, it looked thin and defenceless like a child's. There was a smear of chocolate about her mouth and chocolate wrappings on the floor.

Miss Blackett went to bed early these days. She began the night lying in the centre of the bed, but as soon as she was asleep she instinctively moved to the edge to leave room for Lord Jim. At midnight she half woke, stretched out her hand to stroke him and met nothingness.

One o'clock struck. Mrs Thornton, who was still awake, thought she would try to read herself into drowsiness, and took down the nearest book from her bedside shelf. It was an illustrated copy of Blake's poems, but her old eyes were too tired for reading, so she gazed dully at his pictures instead — the piping boy, the dancing figures beneath the tree, the tiger, till at

155

last she began to doze and dream, though at first it was more of a vivid memory than a dream which took over.

She was a child, or rather she was watching herself as a child, one day when her darling mother had said, "It's really too lovely a morning for school, we'll take the train to Brighton and picnic on the beach." And they had done just this, and there they were at Black Rock with the cliffpath to Rottingdean and the old man with his "Happy Families" box and cap for pennies behind them. Her mother was sitting by a breakwater and she herself, dressed in her favourite white and navy sailor suit, was standing facing the sea at the end of the little stone jetty. Only it wasn't a jetty now but Sir Francis Drake's *Golden Hind* sighting America, and she was, of course, Drake. Mrs Thornton watched the little girl who was herself and Drake, and knew that she was feeling very, very happy. Then her mother called, "Come along, Milly, I've unpacked the basket and there's Gentleman's Relish sandwiches and squashed-fly biscuits," and the child turned round, and though it was still the child she had known so well, the face Mrs Thornton saw was Tom's. But her mother had now changed into old Mrs Langley, who was pouring tea into her beautiful cups beneath the deodar tree. Mrs Thornton, deep in the dream by now, saw that everyone from The Haven was gathered round. She was pleased to see Mrs Langley again and Miss Dawson, too, and Lord Jim prancing about Miss Blackett's feet, but as she looked at Lord Jim, he began to grow. He grew huge, almost as large as a tiger, and his fiery coat flamed in the shade of the great dark branches. Mrs Thornton tried to call out to warn everybody, but she could not make a sound. Lord Jim, still rapidly growing, stepping delicately among Mrs Langley's teacups, was now definitely stalking Leila Ford, who, as he gained in golden power, began, as rapidly, to shrink until she was no more than a pitiful little creature, the size of a wizened child. Mrs Thornton exerted all her strength to move towards her but was quite unable to lift a foot. She was infinitely relieved then when her own Nanny appeared round the tree. "I'll see that the beastie doesna get beyond himself," she said, "and as for Miss Leila, it'll do her a power of good, so dinna fash yourself, Miss Milly." Mrs Thornton could not see what happened next, for a cloud of little birds flew down from the deodar branches and obscured her sight, but with Nanny there she knew all would be in order. The birds were singing loudly, but soon their song turned to instrumental music and there, out in the sunshine on the lawn, were Austen, Elizabeth, Nell and Jake, playing away as hard as they could go. Mrs Thornton was momentarily troubled because she could not recognize the music. Was it Schubert? Was it Mozart? Whatever it was, it was divinely inevitable and, delighted, she drew nearer to the players, and now they glanced round at her and each of them had Tom's wide untroubled stare. At the same time she was aware that the lawn was as crowded as on a fête day. All the village were there and, besides, here and there on the outskirts she thought she caught glimpses of figures in fancy dress, some splendid and some rustic, even a fairy or two — actors, she supposed, come over from Stratford. She looked round for Meg and saw her dancing with one of these, for now everyone was dancing and Mrs Thornton was overjoyed to see about her old friends and relatives, some of whom she had not thought of for years and some she remembered constantly with longing. She was not surprised then when her husband appeared close beside her but she could not help exclaiming, "You will laugh at me I know, but I thought you were dead!" He smiled his old amused affectionate smile and took her hand to lead her into the dance, and, as they whirled round, Tom was everywhere and nowhere, in a glance, in a gesture, in the rhythm of the music.

But then Austen, Elizabeth, Nell and Jake stopped as suddenly as they had begun and a way opened up before Mr

157

Thornton and she saw that "set in the midst of them" was Tom himself. Lord Jim, now his proper size, was draped round his shoulders and he had a pipe in his hands. Mrs Thornton caught herself thinking: "But it was a drum, not a pipe, that he had." But this was only a momentary flashback, for Tom began to play on his pipe and she was caught up by that piping into unalloyed joy. All consciousness of time, place and self ceased, for she was inside the Kingdom.

Then she half woke. She knew she was in bed in her own room but her mind was perfectly blank. She was aware only of peace. She opened her eyes – a wind had risen and dispersed the fog and through the uncurtained window she could see stars. The thought of their multitude, distance and immensity filled her with pleasure and she turned over and went to sleep again.

When she woke the second time, it was full morning and her dream came flooding back. What did it mean? Did it matter what it meant? She remembered that this dream had contained glory, and how could one analyse glory? Through the wall of her room she could now hear Mrs Nicholson's radio broadcasting the first Sunday service of winter time. The resentment she usually felt at any aural invasion of her own territory seemed not to trouble her this morning. She knew that when Mrs Nicholson turned off, as she always did the moment the blessing was pronounced, not waiting for the voluntary, it would be time for her to tune in to her own music programme. The service meant little to her and the music less than nothing to Mrs Nicholson and yet, she supposed, they both really meant the same thing. This unity in variety she now welcomed. What the meaning was she believed she had known for a moment in her dream. The glory had now departed and probably would never come again, but she knew that what it had left her with was a sense of her own blessed irrelevance.